Pleas

Y

Yo

———

KU-452-807

High Bounty at Wayward

When Evangeline Parrish learns her brother has stolen some money, she hires Ransom Fayne, a renowned bounty hunter, to help bring him back before he ruins his life. But the rescue is thwarted by a deadly ambush, and Eva's brother dies and so the mission for Ransom and Eva becomes one of retribution.

The town of Wayward is run by saloon owner Yancy Bodean, who is also leader of the bandit gang. In trying to protect Eva from Bodean, Ransom enlists the aid of an old friend to help cut down the long odds. While there is gold and silver in the nearby hills, it is lead and an unusual hammer of justice which will ultimately determine who lives and dies in Wayward.

High Bounty at Wayward

Terrell L. Bowers

A Black Horse Western

ROBERT HALE · LONDON

© Terrell L. Bowers 2015
First published in Great Britain 2015

ISBN 978-0-7198-1578-2

Robert Hale Limited
Clerkenwell House
Clerkenwell Green
London EC1R 0HT

www.halebooks.com

Typeset by
Derek Doyle & Associates, Shaw Heath
Printed and bound in Great Britain by
CPI Antony Rowe, Chippenham and Eastbourne

CHAPTER ONE

Evangeline Parrish didn't enjoy sitting near the restaurant doorway, especially on a very cool October night. The cold draft caused her to pull her jacket about her shoulders, but there was still a chill to her legs. She accepted the discomfort because the Royal Garden Dining Emporium was the best place in town to eat even though there was frequently a line of people waiting to get in. Her table had been added to try and accommodate another person or two for the overflow from the dining area. But being so close to the entrance and sitting alone at a two-party table presented other problems for an eligible, attractive young lady . . . unwanted prospective suitors or company.

This night, however, there erupted a very different kind of disturbance. Two heavily bearded men entered, carrying sizeable hunting rifles, wearing full-length dusters over dirty woolen shirts and coarse, durable trousers. Their boots were rust-colored from blood splatter and they each wore coonskin headgear over long, greasy hair. They roughly pushed people aside and stormed up to the dining steward. The poor bespectacled man froze in place behind a small altar, wherein he kept a list of names of those who had made special reservations. Fear flooded his features at being confronted by a man twice his size who menacingly shook his fist at him and demanded a table.

'I-I'm sorry, but I cannot seat you,' the small-framed clerk stammered. 'All of our tables are occupied at the moment.'

'You better damn well un-occupy one of them!' the threatening brute snarled.

'We come to eat, skinny,' his pal joined in. 'We provide meat to the railroad and sure don't intend to be wasting our time standing in line.'

The first speaker thrust out his jaw and glowered at the small man. 'You get us a table pronto, or we're gonna tear this fancy place apart!'

George Debar, the maitre d', hurried over to intervene. 'Please!' he beseeched in a politely hushed voice. 'Kind sirs, we have no seating available. If you would care to—'

'Reckon we'll empty out the whole pig pen!' the large man bellowed, cutting him off. 'No bunch of chicken-neck milksops is going to stand in our way, eh, Dead-eye?'

'Right you are, Gunner,' Dead-eye came back at once. 'We'll show these city dudes where to squat!'

Evangeline had been keeping her head down, afraid to look at the brazen encounter, ready to bolt for the door if a fight erupted. Suddenly, a hush fell over the room and she lifted her eyes to see another man had arrived to intervene. She recognized him as the widely known bounty hunter who had arrived in town a week or so ago.

Ransom Fayne had a fixed smile on his face, but spoke so softly she couldn't hear what he said. The two ruffians puffed up at his words and spouted an oath or two, but Fayne silenced their tirade with a simple lift of his left hand. When the bounty hunter spoke again, the pair exchanged an odd, only-a-man-could-understand sort of stare at Fayne. Momentarily, the unruly duo relaxed their hostile postures and seemed to have second thoughts about making a fuss. Each of them took an involuntary step back as though cowed by Fayne's stance.

'I'm sure you understand, fellers,' The renowned tracker's voice was loud enough to be heard this time. 'Any other time, the folks here would be glad to oblige you.'

'Yeah,' Gunner muttered meekly. 'We see how it is.'

'No hard feelings.' Dead-eye was downright courteous.

'Thanks for being understanding, boys,' Fayne told the pair. 'The Grub Shack down the street puts out a passable meal and isn't nearly so crowded.'

Without another word of protest the two men whirled about and strode back out the door. George, visibly relieved at Fayne's handling of the situation, enthusiastically shook his hand and spoke to him in a hushed voice. The bounty hunter said something in return and made his way back to where he had been sitting alone at a table.

Relieved that the impending violence had been averted, a daring thought flashed through Evangeline's mind. As she had not yet been served she rose from her table and boldly went over to George, before he returned to his duties. She explained her notion and he readily agreed. The two of them threaded their way through the crowded dining area and approached Ransom Fayne's table. George quickly made the introductions.

'Mr Fayne,' he began, 'may I present Miss Evangeline Parrish?'

Fayne sat back at the table for two and evaluated her from shoes to hairstyle without ever breaking eye contact. In a gentlemanly reciprocation, he stood up and gave her a polite nod.

'Miss Parrish has made a rather unusual suggestion,' George excused their visit.

'And what is that?' Fayne queried.

'The lady enjoys dining here quite often,' the maitre d' hurried to explain, 'but the – let's call them *would-be paramours* – give her little peace. As you always eat alone, we thought perhaps you would allow her to share your table.'

'I'll understand if you say no,' Evangeline tossed in nimbly. 'But I spend so much time putting off suitors, I'm unable to enjoy my meals.'

'I'm not much for conversation,' Fayne told her bluntly.

'It's tranquility I desire, Mr Fayne. I only wish to eat without the distraction of fawning and intrusive male attention.'

'You've an educated manner of speaking,' he observed appreciatively.

His words of praise caused a rush of heat to wash Evangeline's throat and cheeks. 'My mother was a schoolteacher.'

He lifted a single shoulder in a shrug. 'If you don't mind being seen with someone like me, I'd be right honored to have you share my table.'

George pulled out and held a chair for her. Fayne waited until she was seated before sitting down himself. It was the beginning of an evening dining ritual that, from that day forward, took place several nights each week.

Although it was little more than a quiet meal for the first few times they ate at the same table, once Evangeline became comfortable around the man, she began to make small talk until the food arrived. Before long, she felt confident in telling him whatever was on her mind. It was mostly a one-sided conversation, but dinner together became her favorite part of the day.

The tranquil world in which Evangeline lived changed one Monday morning when she unlocked the door to the Wells, Fargo Express & Transfer company. One step inside the office and an immediate panic swept through her, chilling her to the bone like a bitter wind. The company safe, located behind the customer agent's cage, was ajar.

With her mind and emotions reeling, she spun about wildly, her eyes scanning every corner of the room. Nothing appeared out of place; the door had not been forced open, and the barred windows were secure. Nelly, her elder brother, had worked alone on Sunday, and it was inconceivable that anyone could have entered the office without a key. Kneeling down, she pulled the heavy iron door open and discovered all of the money and gold was missing.

'Morning, sweetheart,' Corwin Hurst's voice greeted from the doorway. 'I thought I would be the first one—'

'We've been robbed!' Evangeline cried. 'The safe is empty!'

Corwin prided himself on being above emotive outbursts, always in control. He was a moderately handsome charmer who had been selected by the Wells, Fargo recruiter to start up the office at Dry Creek, Nevada. He had run the operation for six months without a hitch . . . until today.

'That's impossible!' he wailed, his pomposity displaced by the devastating news. He ran to the safe, looked about the room anxiously and declared: 'The office doors are reinforced with steel and have locks that are superior to anything in this part of the country.' He paused to run his fingers over the locking bolt and sides of the door. 'There aren't any marks on the safe and it doesn't appear to have been jemmied or broken into.'

Evangeline swallowed hard. 'Have you seen my brother since we closed Saturday?'

'The mayor and I went fishing; I didn't stop by the office all day,' Corwin said. 'Do you think someone forced Nelson to open the safe and then kidnapped him?'

'Nothing but the safe was touched. Wouldn't a bandit go through the desk drawers?'

'Surely Nelson wouldn't rob us himself,' Corwin said. Although the words were firm, terror and suspicion entered his eyes. 'Would he?'

'He's been acting strangely,' Evangeline admitted.

'You know he frequently leaves town on his day off and has been very secretive about it. I thought he might have found a girl and just didn't want me to know about her.'

'But robbery?' Corwin whined. 'We've been working together since we opened for business. He was the first man I hired.'

'Only you and he have the combination to the safe,' she pointed out. 'The office was still open when I went to the Royal Garden for supper last night, but I didn't check afterward.'

'This is a nightmare,' Corwin lamented. 'The district manager has been inquiring about our security measures since we had that third stage hold-up last month. I'm hanging on to my position by a shoestring. If your brother stole that money he has cost me my job, and your family will be hounded to repay what he has stolen. You and I are ruined . . . both socially and financially.'

Evangeline rose up and wrung her hands in thought. 'Maybe we can buy some time?' She offered an alternative to jumping off the nearest tall cliff.

'What are you thinking?'

She hurried over behind the counter, then used her key to open a drawer. 'The daily start-up money is in the cash drawer.' She did a quick inspection. 'That means we have a hundred dollars and some change.'

'A hundred dollars won't last long,' Corwin said. 'If someone cashes a banknote or wants to withdraw some of their funds, we won't have enough to cover it.'

'Father has a fair amount of money in the bank at Carson City. Next month is when he usually restocks his inventory. I'll ask him to provide us with enough cash to run the office for a few days.'

'What good will that do?' Corwin asked. 'We have to send a monthly statement of earnings and our cash on hand to the company headquarters in just over two weeks.'

'Exactly,' Evangeline said. 'We can use the time to locate Nelly and get the money back.'

'And if we can't find him or he refuses to return the money? Then what?'

Evangeline frowned. 'Then a warrant will be issued for his arrest, you will be dismissed, and I will be branded as the sister of a thief.'

'Do you really think your father would provide us enough money to keep this office open?'

'Two thousand ought to cover us until the end of the month.'

'How much did Nelson take?'

Evangeline opened her tally book and looked at her last entry. 'Up until yesterday we had a little less than ten thousand dollars in the safe, Mr Hurst.'

'I've asked you to call me by my first name, Eva,' Corwin said. 'We're practically engaged.'

Uncertainty swirled within her chest. 'Nothing has been formally announced yet,' she responded carefully. 'You promised you wouldn't ask for my hand until we had known each other for six months.'

'I *have* known you for six months. That's how long Nelson has been working for me.'

'This isn't the time for discussing romance,' she countered. 'Besides, I didn't move here until some time after Nelly began working for you. I've only been doing bookkeeping and the nightly audits for about three months. We've done very little actual courting, so let's stick to the problem.'

Corwin scowled, but his voice was calm. 'All right, sweetheart, whatever you say.' Then he grunted his disgust. 'But if we can't get the money back, I'm betting your father won't cover the loss.'

'No, he couldn't come up with that much,' she agreed.

Corwin thought aloud. 'The stage from Carson City is due late this afternoon. Even if we get the loan, how are we going to find your brother?'

Evangeline didn't reply to his query. Instead she asked: 'Can Mr Tabor handle this place alone or will you need to stay and help?'

The question caused Corwin's brows to lift. 'What? You aren't thinking that you and I can go after Nelson ourselves, just the two of us?'

'Of course not, but I have to be the one to find him,' she avowed. 'No one else could talk him into returning the money.'

'This country is wide open with a good many lawless towns. We have no idea where he went. How do you propose we find him?'

'I'll hire someone to help us.'

'Hire someone?' He laughed at the idea. 'Who can you possibly hire who knows where to look for your brother? I mean, how much can we pay a hunter or scout, compared to the money Nelson can offer the man when and if we catch up with him?'

'There is a professional tracker in town,' Evangeline

explained. 'He eats at Royal Garden 'most every night. Lately, rather than have me waiting to get a table of my own, he shares his reserved table with me.'

Corwin's face darkened. 'How does he rate a reserved table? And you're telling me you sit down and take your meals with a perfect stranger?'

'No one thinks anything of it, Mr Hurst. The guy hardly ever speaks. Even when I ask a question he grunts the answer like words were gold and he was the worst sort of skinflint. Everyone knows the guy isn't sociable or—'

'You're talking about Ransom Fayne!' Corwin exploded. 'The man's a filthy bounty hunter. How on earth did you end up eating with a man like him?'

Evangeline felt her dander rise at his critical appraisal of a man he had never met. She masked her ire and told him about the first time she had sat with Fayne. She finished by saying, 'And now I simply join him whenever it is busy.'

'And how do you think that looks to everyone in town?'

'It prevents lovesick locals, miners or ranch hands from approaching me. As long as I'm sitting with him I don't have to fight off every would-be suitor in the country. I'm able to eat my meal in peace without anyone bothering me.'

'I've told you that Mother would welcome having you to eat with us. We only have to let her know in advance.'

'I don't wish to be a burden to your mother.'

Corwin fumed. 'And I presume this gunman asks for nothing in return?'

Evangeline gnashed her teeth, but withheld the

14

rancor from her voice or expression. 'The only thing the man does is wait patiently at the table until I finish my meal. He might be a notorious man-hunter, but he is polite and a perfect gentleman. As I explained, he is taciturn and seldom offers a word in conversation.'

Corwin swallowed his jealousy and returned to their predicament. 'To answer your question about Lawrence Tabor, I believe he can manage until we return. I'll give him the safe combination and tell him to put off any complicated contract work or the issuing of large drafts until my return. He knows how to properly clean gold dust before weighing it and how to perform most other operations of the office. It will be hard on him, working every day alone instead of simply helping out a few hours here or there, but we don't really have any choice.'

'Then you agree the best plan is to hire Ransom Fayne and try to get our money back?'

'It would seem the only possible course of action, if we are to save our jobs,' Corwin admitted dourly. 'You get your father to ship the money and I will collect Lawrence and instruct him about his duties.' He paused to dig out his wallet. 'Here,' he handed her several bills, 'I'm sure the bounty hunter will have a better idea of the supplies we'll need for the hunt than you or I.'

'I saw Mr Fayne enter Gibbon's Grub Shack on my way here. As he doesn't socialize, he should be alone at a table. I'll send off a wire to my father, then try to persuade Mr Fayne to help us.'

Corwin reluctantly agreed. Eva tucked the money into her purse and hurried out the door. There was no time to lose.

Evangeline's heart thundered in her chest as she approached Ransom Fayne's table. She had never joined him for breakfast, usually because she got by with a bowl of mush or a pastry from the bakery most mornings. If the man was surprised to see her it didn't show in his makeup. Masculine and capable in appearance, Fayne appeared fresh-shaven, dressed in a spotless Western-style suit: black jacket, pants and hat, polished boots, with an expensive white shirt. Evangeline opined the man to be pleasant and moderately captivating, with neatly shorn black hair and inscrutable dark-brown eyes. Perhaps an inch or two under six foot, he was stalwart, moved with an athletic ease, and oozed a cool confidence without exuding haughtiness or arrogance.

As she made her way over to his table it struck her odd that the notorious bounty hunter was the first man she had ever confided in. Perhaps that was because he was such a good listener, or the fact he never outwardly judged anything she said. Was it possible to have a friendship with a man about whom she knew nothing? Well, nothing other than his reputation. When visiting with him during their meals, she spoke of 'most anything that came into her mind, her dreams for the future or fear of the unknown, even the fact that she had not found a man she felt she could love. The notion of her saying such things to a perfect stranger was silly, absurd, but there had been no discomfort when she disclosed such confidence to him. She knew Ransom would never divulge a word of anything she said to anyone else. Had she been of the Catholic faith, he could have been her priest. The notion struck her as funny and a tenuous smile involuntarily slipped on to her lips.

As was his habit Ransom rose to his feet at her approach. He must have noticed her smile as his demeanor softened noticeably. He remained standing until she sat down across from him. Then, without questioning her presence, he returned to his chair and began to eat the half-finished plate of eggs, ham and toast.

'Mr Fayne,' she began, somewhat breathless from apprehension and the fact she had been rushing around town. 'I need your help.'

Ransom paused from chewing to scrutinize her. Evangeline froze momentarily. Never before, during their many meals together, had the man studied her so openly or frankly. His gaze was more than speculative, it bordered on intrusive, as if he could penetrate her self-protective veneer and delve deep within her very soul. She discovered she was sitting rigid and holding her breath. She felt a warming heat seeping upward to her cheeks and, cowardly, veiled her eyes with her lids in a feeble attempt to halt Ransom's absolute dissection.

'What I mean is,' she blurted out the words, 'I would like to hire you for a job.'

'Hire me.' It wasn't a question, but a mystified statement. 'You do know who I am?'

'Of course I do,' Evangeline replied evenly. 'You're the most deadly bounty hunter in all of the southwest.'

'Actually,' he corrected her, 'the men I *go* after are the most deadly in all of the southwest – killers, defilers, kidnappers or bloodthirsty mongrels who violate the laws of

17

man and God. According to my reputation: out of eleven bounties I've had to kill ten men, and that's not counting a few renegades or hired guns along the way.' He leaned his forearms on the tabletop and asked bluntly: 'Is that really the kind of man you want to hire?'

'I need the best.' Evangeline unwaveringly proceeded with her entreaty. 'This is something that has to happen quickly or it will cost a man his job and ruin the reputation of my entire family.'

Ransom stuck a fork into a slice of ham. 'Go on,' he said simply. 'I'll listen to what you have to say.'

Evangeline recouped her courage and quickly detailed the robbery and the plan she had constituted to forgo informing the hierarchy of Wells, Fargo. She finished by explaining the outcome she expected. 'I'm sure my brother will return the money. Whatever trouble he is in, my father and I will help to set things right.'

'Have you considered the possibility that your brother might be more culpable than you suspect?' At her curious frown, he went on. 'Someone has been tipping off some bandits about your shipments lately.' He narrowed his gaze. 'Three robberies in the past two months, and always when the stagecoach was carrying a large amount of money. Nelson may have been working with those bandits.'

'I'm sure that isn't the case,' Evangeline replied, defending her sibling. 'Nelly wouldn't be involved in something so underhanded and sneaky.'

'Your argument carries little weight,' Ransom countered. 'You just accused your brother of absconding with all of the money from the Wells, Fargo safe. Such behavior is considered by most to be both underhanded and sneaky.'

'I'm sure this was an impulsive act,' Evangeline battled stubbornly. 'By this time he's probably frightened, alone, and wishes he had never taken the money. I'll bet he would love an opportunity to give it back. Especially if he can save his own good name.'

'And what if I catch up with Nelson and he says no?'

Evangeline was jolted back in her chair. She had not even considered that scenario. 'I . . . I suppose we would have to bring him back forcibly to face his crime.'

Ransom did not hide his surprise. 'What do you mean – *we?*'

'I have to go with you.'

It was the first time Evangeline had seen the man actually smile. However, it lacked any warmth or humor.

'Miss Parrish,' he stated emphatically, 'I work alone.'

Evangeline did not back off from her position. 'Don't you see?' she insisted. 'I have to go with you. I'm the only one Nelly will listen to.'

'The muzzle of a .44 stuck up a man's nose can be very persuasive,' Ransom rebutted.

'No!' Evangeline remained adamant. 'Mr Hurst and I must accompany you.'

'Hurst? That limp-wristed daisy?' Fayne laughed his derision. 'He wouldn't last a day on a manhunt like this. I travel from the first light of day until it's too dark to see the ground. During pursuit, the only rest my horse gets is when I walk ahead of him. I eat in the saddle, sleep on the cold ground at nights, and I keep moving until I catch up with my quarry. It's the only way to get the job done.'

19

'Well, Nelly only left last night. He couldn't have more than a few hours' head start. He isn't very hearty or knowledgeable about being on the run, so he shouldn't make very good time.'

'Do you know where he's going?'

'No, but. . . .'

'Did anyone see him leave town?'

'I don't know.'

Ransom snorted contemptuously. 'So we have no way of knowing where to even start looking.'

Evangeline's temper surfaced. 'You're the professional,' she challenged. 'I assumed you would know how to find his trail.'

'Forget for a moment that this plan of yours will be an endeavor of futility,' Ransom said drily. 'How much am I to be paid for my services?'

'Considering we must be back within fifteen days, I can offer you twenty-five dollars a day.' She hurried to add, 'With a bonus, of course, if we get back all of the money.'

Ransom laughed without humor. 'I might consider that proposal if I were going alone. But having to play nursemaid to you and your city-dude boyfriend, then returning a man with a small fortune in gold and coin? I would expect no less than a hundred a day.'

Evangeline coughed from shock. 'A hundred a day?'

'Consider if you will, Miss Parrish, if I wait until Wells, Fargo puts a bounty on your brother, I can collect ten per cent of any stolen money I bring back, plus the reward. If you consider the company offers a minimum of eight hundred dollars for a common road agent, the total would easily add up to over a hundred a day.'

Evangeline was trapped, unwilling to agree, yet unable to say no. She knew her father would foot much of the bill, as he wouldn't want anyone to know his son was a thief. It still seemed an exorbitant fee, but her options were severely limited. Her mouth firmed into a fine line and she hissed the next words through her teeth. 'I might be able to pay a little more. Will you agree to do it . . . for fifty dollars a day?'

'I'm not sure how cordial I can be to your beau for that amount.'

She put on her most sincere look. 'Please, Mr Fayne, won't you help me?'

Ransom heaved a sigh of resignation. 'I can be ready to leave in fifteen minutes.'

She stood up quickly – Ransom rising at the same time. Evangeline removed the money Corwin had given her from her skirt pocket and handed it to him. 'Both Mr Hurst and I will need to rent horses. I'm sure you are better suited to pick out a couple of good mounts. If you would also pick up the needed supplies, I will change into my riding clothes. We will meet you at the livery in thirty minutes.'

Ransom stuck the money inside his jacket. 'Bring along a good blanket and any feminine necessities,' he advised. 'We'll camp by water when it's available, but don't expect any mollycoddling.'

'I understand, Mr Fayne,' she said. 'We will meet you in half an hour.'

CHAPTER TWO

Evangeline discovered that some troubles were akin to being caught in a summer rain shower, one that turned into a downpour and developed into a hurricane. After she had donned her riding-skirt but before she had managed to collect her things, Corwin burst into her room unannounced.

'Evangeline! Miss Parrish!' he cried, waving his arms around wildly. 'We are doomed!'

His terrified screech, with eyes bulging from their sockets, plus his already pallid complexion – more ashen than normal – prevented Eva from admonishing him for entering a lady's chamber without knocking. Hesitant to learn what new difficulty lay ahead, she inquired: 'What is it? What's the matter?'

Corwin gained control of his outpouring and spoke now in hushed tones, as if frightened to speak aloud. 'Wyatt Quigley stopped by while I was going over procedures with Lawrence. He said he would need about half of the money he deposited with us yesterday at the end of the month.'

Evangeline frowned. 'I didn't see an entry for Quigley's deposit.'

'That's just it.' Corwin was practically sobbing. 'He gave the money to Nelson, and your brother didn't write it down in the account ledger. The deposit covered the usual payroll and also the bonuses Quigley is going to pay his miners.'

Evangeline swallowed an unladylike gulp. 'How much money are we talking about?'

'Twenty-two thousand dollars.'

Evangeline gasped, struck numb by the news. She sank down on her bed, her legs no longer able to sustain her weight. This was beyond bad, it was tragic, appalling, unbelievable. Overwhelmed with a fresh despair, she buried her face in her hands and wept.

'Your brother stole over thirty thousand dollars.' Corwin howled his renewed grief. 'We can't hide this from Wells, Fargo. Or the law. We have to tell them about the robbery.' He paced around the room, his voice cracking from emotion. 'It's over,' he lamented. 'Nelson has buried us both.'

Evangeline raised her head and wiped at the tears. 'This is worse than I ever imagined. The company won't forget or forgive losing so much money. Especially after we've suffered three armed robberies in the past two months, hold-ups that have cost the company a lot of money. Nelly was your assistant manager, a man entrusted with the safe combination.' She sighed before adding, 'And Mr Fayne told me that Nelly might be in cahoots with the bandits. He thinks he's the one who was tipping them off as to which stages to hit.'

'The dirty, low down, traitorous rat!' Corwin exploded. 'He played us both for fools.'

'Yes,' Evangeline muttered in defeat, 'it certainly looks that way.'

'It's over,' Corwin said thickly. 'I'll end up working as a bank teller somewhere, or stocking grocery shelves for a living. My whole life is ruined.'

'There is still a chance,' she said, refusing to give up. 'Mr Fayne agreed to help us. I made it clear that we need both my brother and the money returned as quickly as possible.'

'Within our short time-frame, it's asking a lot, even from a bloodhound like him.'

'What do we have to lose?' she returned. 'If we don't catch him your career is over and my family's name is ruined. We are after more money now, but the objective is the same.'

Corwin appeared ready to start pulling his hair out by the roots, but fear of failure and disgrace won out. 'I suppose you're right. Quigley won't be needing his money until the end of the month. If we fail to find your brother and get the money back in time, we can contact Wells, Fargo and I'll tell them about our plan. Then I'll resign from my position.'

'Get your things,' Evangeline told him. 'Ransom will be waiting at the livery stable.'

Ransom gathered supplies for the chase and rented the best two horses the livery had to offer. He was uncomfortable about taking Miss Parrish along, as well as the conceited dandy from the Wells, Fargo office. He should have turned down the condition of their accompanying him and struck out on his own. He could have moved more quickly and had a better chance of catching Nelson before he got out of the country. However, the girl made it quite clear she intended to follow after her brother, which meant she would have hired someone else. An unexpected pang of – what was it? Jealousy? – convinced him that he wouldn't have liked the idea of her turning to another man in this situation.

Nelson and the elderly gent, Lawrence Tabor, were two men he had been watching at Wells, Fargo. He felt certain one of them was in league with the bandit gang, feeding them information as to when the coach would be carrying a goodly sum of money. Tabor spent time at the local casino, but so did Nelson. As for associating with unsavory characters, Nelson seemed to have several drinking buddies, but nothing beyond that.

The hardest part about keeping an eye on him was the fact he could have been conspiring with a number of men. Visitors were allowed to come and go at his boarding house up until well after dark, meaning any of his pals could have been meeting him in his room to plan the robberies. Also, he usually went riding on his day off and didn't return until late or even the next day. That also allowed for him to meet up with someone. The one time Ransom had followed him Nelson rode all the way to Carson City to spend a couple hours at a saloon. He spent a little time talking to a girl or two, but that was all.

As for Tabor, he had a wife, who worked at a dress shop, and a teenage daughter living at home, so he might have been enticed by a way to earn more money.

He only worked a couple days a week. However, a subtle question to Evangeline had revealed that the man didn't have the safe combination. Even so, he could have been privy to when large sums of money were being transported.

Ransom dismissed the express drivers or guards because they seldom knew about irregular shipments – except when extra guards were needed. The bandits had passed on the two or three shipments with heavy guard, so they were picking and choosing their targets – enough cash or gold to make the hold-up worthwhile, yet not so much as to have to deal with added security.

Pausing to look up the street, he saw a man watching the town's activity from a second-story window at the boarding house. That was not unusual, but he looked like one of the fellows Nelson often had a drink or two with. He seemed to be staring in Ransom's direction too, but it might have been the lighting. With the window closed, the sun reflected off the glass.

Evangeline and the agent came hurrying toward the stable and waiting horses, so he concentrated on the present situation. Ransom had grown to enjoy the lady's company on the nights when she took her meal at his table. She would sometimes converse with him seriously, but most often it was about trivial things – her job, the weather, news about someone's new baby. Although he seldom contributed much in return, he relished listening to her. She was attractive, intelligent and charming. He had never made the slightest overture to Evangeline, but it had not escaped his attention that she was quite special. He hadn't really looked at a woman since just after the war. A broken heart took time to heal and he had lost everything he loved in the world, due to his volunteering to fight for the Confederacy. Regardless, he could not deny the attraction he felt for Evangeline. Under different circumstances he would gladly play for the girl's attention. If he didn't make his living with a gun, if he didn't spend all of his time chasing down killers, if his job didn't mean he might be killed at any given moment . . . a lot of ifs.

He ventured forward to meet the pair, took the bundle Evangeline was carrying and quickly secured it behind the cantle of the saddle. She had a few other items that went into the saddle-bags. While Ransom had distributed the supplies to the three animals, he had left room for Corwin and Evangeline's personal things.

'The blacksmith's boy was doing chores and saw your brother pick up his horse last night. He said he headed out of town after dark, going north,' Ransom informed the girl. 'The Central Pacific Railroad has a station at Lake City.'

'You mean Reno, don't you?' Corwin corrected.

Ransom put a hard stare on him. 'Yeah, right,' he said sourly. 'Renamed after a Yank killed at South Mountain during the war.'

'You think that's Nelly's plan?' Evangeline wondered. 'Get to the railroad and then travel back east to get away?'

'You know your brother a whole lot better than I do, Miss Parrish. But a telegraph message to the law over that way to stop him from boarding the train would be a good idea.'

27

'I'll send it straight away,' Corwin said. He made a hasty about turn and trotted back up the street to send the wire.

Ransom watched him for a moment and then checked to see the cinches were tight and everything was packed so it wouldn't rub a sore spot on their mounts. He didn't realize Evangeline had been standing behind him watching until he whirled abruptly about. For a short moment he and the lady were close enough to have been dancing. Although his move had taken her by surprise, she did not back away immediately.

'Uh,' he said uncomfortably, 'these hay-burners often hold their breath, so the cinch needs tightening before you mount up. If it isn't snug, the saddle might turn while you're climbing a hill or something.'

Finally, and with a peculiar sort of reluctance, Evangeline backed up a step and smiled. 'I had a horse like that when I was quite young. My father would always make him walk a bit and then retighten the cinch before I could ride.'

'From what you've told me, I didn't think you were all that close to your pa.'

She made a face – something between indifference or a frown – and admitted, 'That's true. He and Nelly never did get along, and I was more a personal slave than a daughter. Mom died in childbirth with what would have been my second brother. Losing them both hurt my father deeply and he never was quite the same. That's why I followed Nelly here. We both wanted to get away so we could have our own lives.'

'Rich man, your father?'

'Not rich, but his implement shop does a good business in Carson City. He sells farm equipment and all manner of tools. Between the farmers and the miners, he makes a decent living. I borrowed two thousand dollars from him to keep the Wells, Fargo office open, but he will need it back or be forced to take out a mortgage on his place.'

The girl went silent and Ransom glanced up the street, hoping to see Corwin on his way back. Finding he wasn't in sight, he cleared his throat. 'I never asked why you chose to sit down at my table that first time.'

Evangeline uttered a half-laugh at the memory. 'It was cold sitting in that doorway, but it was the only table they had available.'

'Yes, but you didn't know anything about me.'

'I knew you were very capable,' she replied.

'Because I hunt men for a living?'

'No,' she said. 'I was sitting there when those two hunters made such a fuss. I was afraid they would tear the place apart. Then you stepped up and got them to leave without so much as a harsh word.' She gave him a curious look. 'I have often wanted to ask what you said to them.'

'I asked them politely to move along and not cause any trouble,' Ransom recounted.

The girl stared agape. 'That's all it took? You asked them to leave?'

'I suppose they might have gotten the idea that, if they didn't leave quietly, I would gut-shoot them both and feed them to the buzzards.'

Evangeline gazed at him intently, as if trying to decipher if he was making a joke or telling her the honest truth. Regardless, she praised his action. 'Whatever you said, it certainly worked.'

'Got me a reserved table and first-class service every night since, too,' he said, adding with a grin, 'It probably suggests a lack of humility, but I rather enjoy the special treatment.'

The young lady laughed. Her rich brown eyes glowed with delight and the mirth lit up her entire face. Petite features, hair the tawny color of a mule deer, possessing the most delectable mouth Ransom had ever seen. Funny that he hadn't noticed how fetching she was before that moment.

'Yonder comes your beloved,' he said, catching sight of Corwin hurrying down the street. 'Leastways, that's the word he's been spreading around town.'

She grew serious again. 'Yes, Mr Hurst suffers no reservations about his wealth of charm.'

Ransom experienced a mild gratification at her cynical tone of voice, but pushed it out of his mind. Casting an eye at the boarding house, he saw that the man in the window was gone. Probably he'd just been killing time before going to work for the day. He dismissed the idea of being under surveillance: he had a job to do. It would take every bit of his skill to catch up with Nelson and persuade him to return the stolen money before the two weeks were up.

'I should tell you,' Evangeline spoke up. 'Nelly also stole a payroll that was given to him yesterday. Between that money and what was in the safe, he took about thirty thousand dollars.'

Ransom absorbed the information. 'Changes things somewhat,' he said. 'His theft no longer sounds like an impulsive act. Which means he planned this and likely has a destination in mind. Any idea where that might be?'

'Some place,' Evangeline sighed resignedly, 'where there are no lawmen.'

After several hours on the trail Ransom had a keen empathy with a man spreadeagled on an anthill, facing an agonizingly slow and painful death. Listening to Corwin discuss his future plans for Evangeline and himself was sheer torture. The 'me's, 'myself's, and 'I's along with the 'once we are wed's were enough to have driven Moses out of Egypt without freeing his people.

Of course, Ransom could not deny feeling a bit of envy in his misery. Evangeline had never shown an obvious interest in him personally. She had used his reputation to save herself from amorous paramours at the restaurant. A pretty woman never got a moment's peace in a town where the love-starved men outnumbered the females twenty to one. Still, she had been a guest at his table for a great number of meals, and she had asked him to lead this little expedition. That made him special . . . in a primal, insignificant, pet animal sort of way.

'Or we could go to San Francisco,' Corwin rambled on. 'I know a banker there who would hire me in a heartbeat. It would take a year or two, but I'm sure it wouldn't be long before I was moved up to an executive position.'

Evangeline had remained generally silent since leaving Dry Creek. Ransom was about to plead with

Corwin to cease the relentless, inane chatter when he discovered the horse he'd been following had suddenly veered off the trail. He immediately pulled his mount to a standstill. The action caused an interruption to Corwin's yammering and the young lady promptly came up alongside him.

'What is it, Mr Fayne?' she asked.

Ransom stared off in the direction the rider had taken. 'Looks like your brother took a detour.'

'Reno is the other way, isn't it?'

'That's right,' Ransom replied. 'The closest place in his new direction is a mining town off to the southeast, and a major trail that leads over into Utah. It looks as if Nelson isn't en route to a train station.'

'Then he must not be planning to run as far.'

'Hard to know what's on his mind,' Ransom replied, trying to figure the man's route. 'If he's headed to the cross-country trail, he might be going to Utah, Idaho or even Arizona. There's hundreds of miles and an endless number of towns once he crosses the border.' He swung about and gazed at Evangeline. 'Can you think of any destination he might have in mind?'

'I have no idea,' she answered. 'Nelly never talked to me about wanting to move or go anywhere. I thought he was happy just being away from Father.'

'He must know about the main trail, if he is leaving the marked route. I'd say we are a couple miles this side of Rock Miner's Road, that's the main trail I was talking about. The nearest town is Wayward. It's a thriving set-tlement that sits along the stagecoach route.'

'What's your brother up to?' Corwin asked, having

moved up to join them. 'How could he possibly know about these back country trails?'

'He often went riding on his day off,' Evangeline informed him. 'Sometimes he didn't get back until late at night or even the next day. I asked him about it a time or two, but he would shrug and say he just wanted to get away from town. He never said anything about meeting anyone or looking over the country.'

'I'm beginning to think Nelson kept a lot of secrets from you,' Ransom said.

Evangeline's response was languid. 'We never were very close. The main thing we had in common was a tyrant for a father.'

'I'm surprised the man loaned you the money to keep the Wells, Fargo office open.'

'Oh, yes,' she snickered. 'At ten per cent interest and a promise we pay him back by the end of the month.'

'A father's love for his children,' Corwin quipped. 'Were my father alive, he would have given us everything he had and offered to help run the place until we returned.'

Evangeline looked at Ransom. 'What about your father?'

'He was a principled man, who believed everyone was responsible for their own actions,' he replied. 'My father would have told me to man up, tell the truth and take the consequences.'

Corwin scowled at the insinuation he wasn't acting the part of a man. He spoke up to cover his irritation. 'You used the past tense,' he mentioned. 'Does that mean your father is no longer alive?'

'My entire family died shortly after the raid at Lawrence, Kansas.'

Evangeline's demeanor reflected an instant compassion. 'You mean they were killed during Quantrill's raid?'

'No, from retribution by a few rogue Yankee sympathizers. They shot my father and burned down our house. My mother and little sister were hiding inside.' He could not mask the pain and bitterness that still raged inside his chest. 'I was off serving with the Confederacy at the time.'

'How very sad.'

Ransom displayed a grim smile. 'That's me, a three-time loser. Lost the war, lost my family, and even lost my girl. While I was off fighting, she married a coward who refused to join either side.'

'Let's hope your luck has changed.' Corwin made a jest. 'Otherwise, we might end up as unwelcome guests in a hostile Indian camp.'

'I'm sure, if you knew the language, you would talk them to death and save our hides,' Ransom retorted.

Evangeline gasped. 'Mr Fayne!' She whirled in the saddle to stare at Ransom. Corwin was, for the first time since this trip began, at a loss for words. Both waited for the bounty hunter to retract the insult or offer some form of appeasement.

'We best keep moving,' was Ransom's vapid response. 'Nelson probably feels secure enough not to try to hide his trail. If he gets careless it might allow us to overtake him.'

Rather than criticize him for his discourtesy toward

Corwin, Evangeline let the matter drop and returned to their original quest. She observed, 'I still find it hard to believe that Nelly has some diabolical plan.'

'I'd say he has proved as much to be the case, Miss Parrish.'

Evangeline recommended, 'Considering the amount of time we've spent together, and the fact this chore might take days or even weeks, you don't have to be so formal. Call me Eva.'

'Be right honored for the courtesy,' Ransom reciprocated. 'I prefer Rance or Fayne myself.'

'All right, Rance,' Eva responded, displaying a coy smile. 'Any ideas as to what my brother could be planning?'

'It's likely Nelson is the one who has been giving out the information on your shipments of gold and cash. If so, it means he is working with a bandit gang. We might be after more than just one man.'

'B-but . . .' Corwin stammered. 'Nelson? Working with bandits?' He shook his head vigorously. 'I mean, the drivers reported six or more highwaymen on each of those hold-ups. We could be riding into a trap and facing a dozen gunmen.'

'It's possible,' Rance admitted. 'The man has planned this caper cleverly to this point. If I was him, I'd have a couple men watching my back trail.'

Corwin was holding back his reins so tightly, his horse started to back up. 'We can't take on a small army of men. I didn't come after Nelson to end up dead in this wilderness.'

'You can return home if you wish,' Eva advised. 'You

needn't risk your life; he's my brother. All you have to lose is your job, and there's a chance the company won't fire you over this theft.'

The minute amount of courage that Corwin possessed surfaced. 'I can't let you go alone. I mean, we are practically engaged.'

'I told you this morning that such a statement is premature, Mr Hurst. I wouldn't want you risking your life when our relationship might turn out to be mere friendship.'

'*Mr Hurst!*' he complained. 'And you and this bloodhound are on a first-name basis?'

Eva did not mask a dark scowl. 'Very well, *Corwin*. We shall all be on a first-name basis.'

'Time's a-wasting,' Ransom butted in. 'As the situation has changed, it might be best if neither of you were along. If it comes to a gunfight, I don't want to be worrying about anyone's hide but my own.'

'You're not getting rid of me that easily.' Eva remained steadfast. 'I still believe there's a possibility of saving my brother from being on the run for the rest of his life.'

Rance advised, 'This might be more dangerous than I first thought. You really should reconsider and let me go it alone.'

Eva chose to ignore his warning and queried, 'If my brother was going east, why not take the road leaving town on the southern route? It would have been a much shorter distance.'

'I reckon he came this way to throw off any pursuit. I'm probably the only man in fifty miles who could have picked up his trail. A posse would have certainly figured he was going to Reno and continued on the main road.'

She uttered a despondent sigh. 'I had so hoped this was an irrational act, a mere happenstance, due to finding so much money ready at hand. But if it's true, if Nelly was in league with the men doing those stage hold-ups too. . . ? I fear the only thing awaiting him is a long prison sentence.'

'There can't be any doubt someone was passing information to those bandits.'

A look of resolve clouded her pretty face. 'I won't go back,' she persisted. 'If I can talk to Nelly, I still might be able to persuade him to return the money. He has to listen to reason.'

'I'm not exaggerating the danger,' Ransom warned her. 'I would never forgive myself if anything happened to you.'

'He's my brother,' she reaffirmed. 'It's my family's honor at stake. I refuse to quit without making every possible effort.'

'I'll find him and bring him back to you.'

'Nelly might not give up to you without a fight. I don't want him hurt.'

Ransom firmed his jaw to keep from debating further. Arguing with a woman seemed about as fruitful as butting heads with a bull . . . all it got a man was a headache. He'd do his best to make sure she stayed under cover if it came to a shoot-out. That was about all he could do.

'Fine,' was his final word on the subject. He touched his heels to his mount and left the main trail, following after Nelson. The man still had six or eight hours' head start so they would not catch up with him today unless he stopped.

The late-afternoon sun glowed dimly through a gathering of ominous-looking clouds when the trail led Ransom and his small party along a hogback ridge. The pathway was narrow, lined with scrub oak, a few trees and scattered patches of grass or wild flowers. The air was unusually still, with no birds chirping and not a squirrel or chipmunk moving through the brush. The quietude caused a raising of the hair on Ransom's arms. He strained his eyes and his ears, trying to penetrate the foreboding silence, searching for unseen danger.

Deciding to to have Eva and Corwin stop and wait so he could have a look around, he turned abruptly in his saddle. The movement came at the exact same moment as two gunshots. Something hit him a glancing blow in the upper torso and another jolt slammed into the pommel of his saddle.

Instinctively, Ransom rolled off his horse in the direction he had been turning. The problem with the unplanned dismount was his being on the sheer side of the ridge. He hit the steep slope and slid and tumbled downward, rolling and falling until he bounced off a tree. The contact caused his body to be flipped to one side and then continue down the shale and rock incline all the way to the debris-littered bottom of the ravine.

With his breath gone, his head spinning, and no way to evaluate how badly he had been injured, Ransom battled a mental fog while he lay completely still. From up the hill he heard men's voices and Eva's cry of fear and despair. His brain told him to jump to his feet, scramble up the mountainside and defend the very special lady. Unfortunately, his body lacked the capability to pry open his eyelids.

Maybe, when my head clears, he told himself. *I'll rescue her once I regain my strength . . . providing I don't wake up standing in the daunting presence of the Lord!*

CHAPTER THREE

There were six of them, men using their bandannas as masks, all with guns drawn. They swarmed about and overwhelmed Eva and Corwin. One man grabbed the reins to Ransom's horse. At the same time, hoods fashioned from a heavy black cloth were hastily fitted over Eva's and Corwin's heads. Next, their hands were bound behind their backs. None of the ambushers spoke and the two captives were soon being led along the trail.

'Who are you?' Eva risked asking. 'Why did you shoot Mr Fayne? Did you kill him?'

'Enough with all the damn questions, woman!' growled a man with a severely deep voice. 'You best worry about your own hide.'

The ride seemed long due to the captives suffering remorse and fear, and the infernal silence among their captors. The man who had warned her must have been the leader as he was the one to call a halt to their journey. In actual time, Eva guessed it had not been more than thirty minutes since the attack. She assessed that much by being able to look directly downward and tell that the sun had not yet set.

After a few moments a pair of rough hands grabbed her by the waist and she was dragged out of the saddle. Eva blinked and coughed at the dust from the inside of the dirty hood as the man lifted it up enough for her to see.

'Keep your eyes to the front,' the leader warned. 'If you see my face I'll have to kill you.'

Eva followed orders and discovered they had come to an old mine, complete with a wooden shanty and two different abandoned holes. One was bored into the side of the mountain and appeared to have been dug for twenty or thirty feet. The second had a huge pile of dirt next to it and was encircled by a three-foot-high, single-pole fence, indicating the dig went straight down. Her captor guided her over to the railing. She began to resist, fearful he meant to toss her into the shaft.

'Ease up on your brakes, woman,' the bass-voiced man jeered. 'You only got to take a look down in the hole.'

Eva ceased struggling and continued to the rim, where he stopped her at the safety fence. She leaned forward and peered into the shaft. There, perhaps twenty feet down, at the very bottom and lying in a twisted heap, was the body of her brother.

'No!' she cried. 'Nelly!'

'Your brother tried to deal from the bottom of the deck with us,' the man said harshly from behind her. 'We had a good thing going. He was selling us the information about when the stage was carrying a lot of money, but he got greedy. He didn't know we had a man in town

41

watching him. When he sneaked out with his belong-
ings, we knew he was up to something. Turns out he was
going to end our arrangement by stealing a whole lot of
money and disappearing.'

She sniffed back her tears. 'You didn't have to kill
him.'

'Well, that was your doing, woman.' He put the blame
on her. 'You went and hired that bounty hunter, Fayne.
Hell's bells!' There was awe in his voice. 'No one in his
right mind wants to have that guy on his trail. Nelson was
a liability, a man who would be recognized. That's why,
instead of just forcing him to share his loot, we had to
kill him.'

'What are you going to do with us?'

'Killing a woman ain't well thought of in these parts,'
he answered. 'You and your pal will be tied up and spend
the night at this cozy little cabin. By the time you get
loose we will be fifty miles away. From the looks of it,' he
paused, evidently looking skyward, 'there's a storm on its
way. That means our sign will be washed away and no
one will be able to track us. We can set up a new business
venture in Wyoming or Colorado, or maybe someplace
else. It doesn't matter. You and the law won't have a clue
as to where to find us and no one knows what we look
like.'

Eva stared down at Nelson. 'Won't you let us bury my
brother?'

'We didn't throw him in a hole just to hoist his carcass
back up,' the man replied gruffly. But then he mellowed
somewhat. 'Tell you what we will do. Seeing as he was our
partner in crime, we'll toss down enough dirt and rocks

to cover him up. If you want more than that, you can figure a way to get his body out of that hole.'

The sack came back over her head and she and Corwin were led inside the cabin. She was blinded by the hood and wrinkled her nose at the smell of decayed wood and dust. Pushed down to a sitting position on the dirt floor, Corwin sat with his back against hers and they were bound tightly together with a length of rope.

'Like I said,' the crusty-voiced man spoke, once they were secured, 'we'll bury your brother, but we ain't gonna say no words over him. Be rather disrespectful, considering we're the ones responsible for his demise.' He laughed. 'You can pray for his soul once you get loose.'

'You've tied us up awfully tight,' Corwin whined. 'What if we can't get free?'

The man snickered. 'In that case, you'd better hope you starve before the coyotes or a hungry bear finds a way into the shack.'

That was the end of the conversation. The door closed and a few muffled words could be heard from the men outside. Next, Eva detected the sound of them tossing rocks and dirt into the shaft. After a short while the horses left the yard.

'So much for hiring the best man-hunter in the country,' Corwin sounded off. 'No warning for us at all and Fayne never got off a single shot.'

Eva sighed, thinking of the seemingly infallible gunman. She had gotten him killed. It was her fault. Nelly had been selling information to a bunch of bandits and had then cleaned out the safe and stolen a payroll.

She should have accepted that he had gone bad, that he had no conscience or love for her and their father. His actions had ruined all of their lives and ended with his own death.

What a fool I've been, she communed silently. *Please, God, tell Rance I'm sorry.*

Rance opened his eyes to discover it was dusk. He was groggy, covered with dust and weeds, had the taste of dirt in his mouth, and there was a ringing in his ears. However, it was the sound of voices from somewhere up on the ridge that roused him to full consciousness. He spat to clean his mouth and began to test his muscles and limbs. He had a good many bumps and scrapes, but nothing seemed to be broken.

Rising to a sitting position, he examined the wound on his right side and discovered it to be a graze along his ribs. It wasn't deep and had already stopped bleeding. Turning in the saddle at the exact moment the shooters fired had saved his life.

Rance reached down with his hand and found his gun was still in place. Carefully and quietly he began to crawl along the bottom of the wash. He came upon an animal trail and followed it up the side of the hill. When he reached an outcrop of boulders he eased in between three large rocks and waited patiently.

'Why do I have to go down there?' A man's voice floated through the dense air.

' 'Cause Joe told you to make sure Fayne was dead,' said a second man.

'If he wanted us to check on him, he should have said

so right off. Why did he wait until after we grabbed the other two and rode all the way to the cabin?' The man swore. 'It's too dark to see where the body landed.'

'Gripe, gripe, gripe, you big baby,' a third voice entered the conversation. 'We'll go with you and hold your hand. Tie off your cayuse and let's get this over with.'

Rance could make out three shadows sky-lighted atop the ridge. He watched as they moved a few feet, then took the most accessible pathway down the hill. Removing his gun, he checked the action to make sure nothing had been damaged by his fall. Everything worked, so he stealthily wormed his way to a better position, one where he could be above the trio when they reached the wash.

'You sure this is where he fell?' one of them asked.

The reply was curt. 'Open your eyes, stupid. Can't you see the marks from where he slid and rolled down the hill?'

'Oh, yeah,' the man he'd called stupid replied. 'He's gotta be right below us. Best keep our guns handy in case he ain't done for.'

'I got him clean,' one bragged. 'Seen the bullet hit him right in the gut.'

'Well, I had to shoot uphill a little,' the second shooter admitted, 'but we sure enough knocked him out of the saddle. If he didn't die right away, he's done for by this time.'

Rance let them come. They passed within fifteen feet of his hiding-place and started a cautious descent down the sheer bank into the bottom of the wash. That was as far as they got.

'Hold it right there,' Rance ordered. Poised in a crouch, he had his gun aimed at the trio.

The three instantly whirled toward him, weapons out, ready to fire.

Rance, primed and set on solid ground, had the advantage. The three ambushers were on a slippery slope with uncertain footing. It made for a hard shot, especially when they had to turn almost all the way around while trying to avoid shooting one another.

Rance's first round knocked one man off his feet. Rapidly he fired again, taking out a second gunman before either of them got off a shot. The third man blasted away with two wild shots. One bullet screamed off the nearby rocks and the second hit somewhere near Rance's feet. A steady aim and deadly accuracy put a bullet through the last man's chest. He buckled at the waist and tumbled into the gully after his two sidekicks. In less than a heartbeat for each, the three ambushers had been cut down.

Rance kept watch for a few seconds after the dust settled. One uttered a dying groan and another twitched convulsively, then all movement and sounds ceased. He kept his gun ready as he made his way over to check on them. It was an unnecessary precaution, as there wasn't a breath of life left in any of the bandits.

'You bushwhack a man, you best make sure he's dead before you walk up on him,' he told the muted, would-be killers. 'Some men don't take kindly to getting shot from ambush!'

*

It took most of the night before Eva could work one of her wrists free and was able to untie herself and release Corwin. It was full dark and, being uncertain of where they were, they decided to wait until daylight to leave the cabin. After a fitful couple hours and unable to do more than doze for a few minutes, Eva at last got up and tested the door. It was not locked or barricaded, so she pushed it open and ventured out as far as the mine-shaft. Dark clouds were overhead and the scent of impending rain wafted in the gentle breeze that rustled through nearby tree limbs and leaves. Corwin came up alongside her to stand at the edge of the black pit. After a prolonged silence he cleared his throat.

'At least they covered Nelson's body.'

'Yes.' Eva was solemn and reverent. 'I said a silent prayer for him.'

Corwin turned to their current situation. 'They took our horses, so we're going to have a long walk in the rain. That is, unless you want to wait out the storm in the cabin.'

'We've no food or water. I think we'd better get started out of these hills.'

'Unless a wagon or someone comes along after we reach the main trail, we won't make it to Dry Creek in one day.'

'I'm open to ideas,' Eva said. 'But surviving on insects and grubs is not one of them.'

'Looks like this was a wasted trip.' Corwin spoke in a pungent tone. 'Fayne and your brother both dead; I'll likely get fired; and I'm sure they won't keep you on at the company, either.'

'Poor Nelly,' she murmured. 'He never wanted to be a workhorse like Father. He was always looking for an easier way to make a living. I never dreamed he would stoop to robbery to get ahead.'

'At least he won't be publicly ridiculed and sent to prison,' Corwin remarked. 'That will save your father a degree of humiliation.'

Tears began to slide down Eva's cheeks. 'I feel terrible . . . not only about Nelly, but Mr Fayne too. I begged him to take this job and got him killed.'

'He was a bounty hunter.' Corwin dismissed her sympathy. 'He'd likely have ended up lying at the bottom of some gully, even if he hadn't come with us.'

'Corwin!' she snapped. 'You can be such a . . .'

The words died in her throat. Not more than a hundred feet away, a single rider and three horses appeared on the trail. It was light enough to see the man clearly and it brought an inhalation of surprise to her lips.

'Rance!' she cried. 'I don't believe it.'

Rance continued forward until he was a few feet away from the pit. Then he stopped the horse and dismounted stiffly. To his surprise – and distinct pleasure – Eva ran over to him and hugged him tightly. He grunted as she pressed against his tender ribs and she immediately jumped back.

'You've been shot!'

'Not much more than a scratch.' He dismissed the wound. 'I doused it with a little whiskey I found in one of the bandit's saddle-bags and improvised a bandage.'

Eva took notice that the horses were not their own.

'What?' She stared at Rance in wonder. 'But how did you. . . ?'

'What happened? Where did the bandits go?' Rance inquired. 'Did they just leave you here afoot?'

'Something like that,' Eva said. Then she explained about her brother being dead and she and Corwin being left bound up in the cabin. She finished with, 'We managed to get free, but with no horses and not knowing where we were, we had to wait for daylight.'

'The gang said they were leaving the country,' Corwin joined in on the story. 'With the rain coming at 'most any minute, there won't be any trail to follow.'

'They will almost certainly send someone back to find out what happened to the gents who belonged to these horses.'

Corwin gaped. 'You mean you killed three of them?'

'Seemed the only way to finish the job I started.'

'But we saw you shot,' the man babbled inanely. 'And you plunged over the side of a cliff. How did you manage to kill three bandits after that?'

'They can't be too far ahead.' Eva ignored Corwin's incredulity. 'They left in the dark, but they surely intended to meet up with the men they sent to check on you.'

'You two should head for home,' Rance said to the girl. 'Your brother is dead, so your being along no longer serves a purpose. Plus, it might take a long time to run down the rest of this gang.'

'There were at least six of them who grabbed us,' Eva said. 'You killed three, but the driver of the stage claimed there were seven or eight on one of the robberies. We

49

might not have seen them all.'

'It makes no difference, ma'am. I've got a job to do.'

'It's Eva, not *ma'am*,' she corrected him. 'And you are in no shape to do this alone.' She hurried on with her argument. 'I can tend the animals and do the cooking. If it comes to a fight, I'm a passable shot with a rifle.'

Rance threw up his hands. 'Hold on, woman! I can't take you with me and risk your life again. You two are darn lucky to be alive.'

'They killed my brother, Rance. If you won't take me with you, I'll find somebody else who will.'

'Best start looking,' he said.

'I'm too close to stop now,' she retorted. 'I'm going after those murderers from here. If you don't let me ride with you, I'll follow you.'

'Don't be ridiculous, sweetheart,' Corwin interjected. 'Bounty hunting is not a chore for a proper lady.'

'Shut up, Corwin!' Rance and Eva said in unison.

Eva nearly smiled at Corwin's startled expression, but hurried on with her case. 'If those men reach a settlement or something, I can ask questions without arousing suspicion.' She hurried forth with the debate. 'And no one would suspect a woman, if we had to keep watch on one of the bandits, while waiting for him to lead us back to their hideout.'

Rance groaned. 'I suppose the only thing I can do is escort you two back to town.'

'No!' Eva cried. 'I won't go! Those filthy snakes tried to kill you and they murdered my brother. I'm not about to forget that. If you're not going after them, I'll start searching for them on my own.'

'You'd be lost within a mile,' Rance said. 'Besides which, you have no food or supplies.'

'There must be a trading post or something near here. You said there was an important trail a few miles away, going east and west. And there's the town you mentioned, too.'

Rance flicked a glance at Corwin, but the man had been cowed by the two of them telling him to shut up. He had only one interest and that was getting back home as fast as he could. There was a good possibility the bandits would send a rider back to see what had happened to the three dead men. If a decision wasn't made quickly, that might add a degree of danger to the return trip.

'All right.' Rance gave in. 'But you will do exactly as I say from this point on without question.' He waited until Eva nodded her head in accordance with the demand, then put his attention on Corwin.

'You take a horse and stick to this path until you hit the ridge where we were attacked. From that point on, keep up a good pace until you are out of the hills. You should make Dry Creek by late this afternoon.'

Corwin hesitated and looked at Eva. 'Evangeline, are you sure about this?'

'Get going, Corwin,' she said firmly. 'I'll be fine. Report what has happened to Wells, Fargo and make sure my father gets his money back . . . with interest. I'm sure Wells, Fargo will take care of everything.'

'Yeah,' he muttered. 'Including my dismissal.'

'I'm sorry for what my brother did,' Eva said. 'I sincerely hoped we could get him to return with the money.'

51

Corwin didn't reply further or hesitate. He mounted up and disappeared down the lane. Eva showed relief that he had gone and looked at Rance, awaiting his orders.

'There is some hardtack in the saddle-bag of my horse. Grab a couple biscuits and we'll get started.' Rance lifted his eyes and checked the clouds. 'We haven't much time before the storm hits. We need to confirm the direction the riders are going. Once it starts to rain, the tracks will disappear and we'll have to guess their destination.'

Eva started for the saddle-bag on the horse he had been riding, but stopped to look him squarely in the eye. 'You won't be sorry for taking me along, Rance. I promise.'

Rather than tell her he was already sorry, he began to remove the rain gear from the dead men's bedrolls.

Rance, old boy, he admonished himself, *you are a sucker for a pretty face. Next thing, you'll be picking wild flowers or buying Eva a box of candy!*

Joe Marcone entered the Wayward saloon and spotted his partner, Yancy Bodean, sitting alone at a card table drinking a cup of coffee. He strode over, pulled out a chair and sat down.

'We've got a problem, boss,' Joe stated grimly.

'What's that?'

'Needle, Sal and Digger ain't come back yet,' he said. 'I thought they might have arrived late and gone straight to bed. I didn't know they were missing till I went and checked their bunks. Then I looked for their horses at the livery. No one has seen them.'

Yancy sat forward, immediately concerned. 'How could that be? Didn't both Digger and Sal claim to have put slugs into that bounty hunter's chest?'

'Fayne was knocked out of the saddle, went boots over tin cup down the side of a mountain and landed in a gully. We all figured he was done for.' Joe heaved a deep breath of air. 'I should have sent a man down to check on him right away, but didn't think there was any need. Needle is the one who suggested we ought to make sure the tracker wasn't found. Trouble is, he didn't say nuthin' until when we had our two prisoners up to the deserted cabin. Damn, boss, I sent the three of them back to check on Fayne, before we left to make the false trail toward Reno. I can't figure what went wrong.'

'You better have someone go find out what happened. If Fayne is still alive we will have to keep a sharp watch for him.'

'I've got Junior and a couple of the boys putting on their slickers. It'll be a wet ride before they can reach that razor-back ridge.'

'We have to know where those men are,' Yancy maintained. 'Do you think your brother can handle this?'

'He'll have Red Dog with him, in case they have to do any tracking,' Joe said. 'It shouldn't take them more than a couple hours to sort this out.'

Yancy sent Joe on his way and called over the guy who managed the casino tables and most of the hired help. Chuck Lefever had worked in saloons for twenty years and relished being finally in a position of authority.

'You need something, Mr Bodean?'

'We might have a security problem, Chuck. I want you to put an extra guard or two on duty until further notice.'

'What are they to watch for?'

'There's a dangerous bounty hunter, name of Ransom Fayne,' Bodean explained. 'He could come here looking for trouble.'

'You got it.'

'Make sure to mention the same warning to the girls and bartender when they start work,' Yancy directed. 'If the man shows up, I want to deal with him quietly. No trouble in the casino.'

'Sure, I understand. Wouldn't want everything getting busted up in a brawl or something.'

'Thanks, Chuck.'

'You'll be in your room or office then?' the man inquired.

'Yes, probably in my upstairs office, where I can keep an eye on things.'

'I'll get those guards on duty right away.'

'Good man,' Yancy praised him. 'I'm glad you agreed to come to work for me.'

Chuck laughed. 'At the salary you offered? I'd have been crazy not to take the job.'

Yancy watched the man round up a couple of employees and instruct them. One hurried from the saloon and another went up to visit the girls' rooms. He tapped his fingers nervously on the tabletop and stared at his cold cup of coffee.

It seemed unlikely, but that miserable man-hunter, Fayne, must have survived. Still, could he have killed three armed men after being shot and left to die? It made no sense. Joe said the shooters were less than a hundred feet away and both were using Winchesters. How could they have missed?

Yancy cast off his curiosity. The plan had not worked to perfection, but the casino was flush at the moment. He had plenty of money to finish buying the final few things he wanted. Miners had begun to pass the word that Wayward's new saloon/casino was open. And they had girls! Only three so far, but two more were on their way, and Belle was a passable singer. He also had a good piano player. Once he started scheduling traveling road shows – theater groups, singers, dancers and other enter-tainers – his stage would be alive with music, song or drama 'most every night. One thing he had learned, it took money to make money. So far, he had the finest bar and decor of any saloon within a hundred miles. Three different mines in the area, a couple big ranches, and the place was located on the main stagecoach or traveler route to Reno and the railroad. Yep, everything was going as planned ... except for one lousy bounty hunter!

CHAPTER FOUR

Corwin muttered a string of oaths as he rode down the soggy mountain trail. His world had gone from bright and sunny to being as miserable as the infernal rain that pelted his oil slicker. A growing pillar in the community, the most eligible bachelor in Dry Creek, he had a promising career and the possibility of one day advancing to the position of district manager with Wells, Fargo. Add to that, he had been one step away from having Evangeline Parrish on his arm and making her his wife. Money, power, esteem, the prettiest woman in town – it was all gone. Nelson had ruined his life, destroyed everything Corwin had earned and achieved with one traitorous act!

And what of his soon-to-be-betrothed? Didn't she realize how this would look to everyone in town? She was gallivanting around the countryside with a crazed bounty hunter, riding at his side and spending her nights sleeping next to him without a chaperone. What respectable woman would do something like that? It was scandalous, downright immoral, and he would make

sure the people around town learned about her inde-
cent ... nay, *illicit* behavior! Desert him for a lowlife
gunnie, would she, a disreputable man-hunter who
made his living by killing or chasing after criminals –
he'd show her! He would make her a pariah, a disgrace
to society. She would never dare show her face in Dry
Creek ever again.

Stopping his horse, Corwin blinked at the rain that
sprinkled his face, gathering his bearings. The beaten
path had led him back to the more readily traveled trail
where he and Evangeline had been taken hostage. He
had arrived at the ridge where the initial attack had
taken place. With a dejected sigh, he started his horse
moving again. So busy was he cursing the weather,
Nelson Parrish, and the ill turn of fate, he didn't see the
two men on the trail ahead until they were but a few
yards away. Corwin yanked on the reins and attempted to
turn his horse around.

Too late!

Another two riders swooped out of nowhere to block
his retreat. For the second time in as many days, he
found himself surrounded by several men on the narrow
ridge trail.

'Well, if it ain't the Wells, Fargo agent,' an unshaven,
mean-looking individual sneered. 'How do you happen
to be riding Digger's horse?'

'D-Digger?' Corwin stammered, realizing these were
likely some of the same men who had kidnapped them
the previous day. 'I don't know anyone called Digger.
This horse was running free. I caught him after being
taken hostage and left bound up in an old miner's cabin.'

'What do you know about the three men lying dead at the bottom of this here hill?' the most youthful-looking one of the group asked.

'I don't know anything,' Corwin mumbled weakly. His pulse pounded loud and hard and fear burned within his chest. 'Like I said,' he hurried on with his story, 'me and a young lady spent the night tied up in a shack. After we got loose, she stayed at the cabin while I started walking toward Dry Creek. I stumbled on this horse wandering unattended. If . . . if Digger is around, I'll certainly pay him for the use of his horse.'

'Dad blame, Junior,' the sinister-looking man guffawed, 'this city dude don't lie for shucks.'

'I'll make you a one-time offer, Mr Agent man,' Junior said. 'You tell us the complete truth about what happened and we will let you go.' He snorted. 'O'course, you can't take Digger's steed, 'cause that would make you a horse-thief.'

'Uh, well . . .' Corwin trembled, hysteria beckoning. Somewhere, from deep inside, he gathered enough bravado to ask, 'How do I know you won't kill me?'

Junior grinned, but there was no friendship in his expression. 'We are leaving the country, mister. We got to wondering why our pals hadn't shown up, so we come back for a look-see. Damned if they ain't all three dead-er'n your boot leather. We want to know how they ended up that way.'

Corwin didn't trust the man, but his lone option was talk or be tortured. He had never engaged in fisticuffs or grappling, because he had no tolerance for pain . . . especially his own. He quickly blurted out the story of

Fayne showing up with the three horses and the decision for him to return to Dry Creek.

'So that troublesome female and Fayne are still in pursuit?'

'I tried to talk her out of it,' Corwin insisted. 'I mean, how does it look – a proper young lady riding with a bounty hunter? Eating and sleeping on the trail together? It's downright sinful.'

'Women today,' Junior said, with a knowing shake of his head. 'They've got no shame.'

'I want no more to do with her or chasing after the company's money. That's why I'm returning to Dry Creek.'

'Dismount and start walking,' Junior ordered. 'We'll be taking the horse with us.'

Corwin got down quickly. He glanced upward at Junior, squinting through the rain. 'Then I can go?'

'Yup,' Junior said nonchalantly. 'I believe you've told us the truth.'

Corwin turned and began to walk down the trail. He managed only two steps before a jolt hit him like a hammer between the shoulders. The echo of a gunshot, muffled by the low-hanging clouds and driving rain, rang in his ears. Corwin's brain scrambled to understand what had happened. His face was in the mud, and yet he had no strength to lift his head.

'Shove him over the edge, Ace,' Junior's voice reached his ears. 'He can join Digger and the others.'

Corwin had not yet lost consciousness when he felt the toe of a boot against his ribs. His body was nudged off the trail and he slid down the side of the soggy slope.

After the first few feet Corwin's world turned black and silent. There was no pain, no awareness that his body was plunging down to a watery, rocky grave. He felt nothing at all.

The tracks were becoming blurred by the downpour of rain. Rance had kept up a fast pace, hoping to reach a crossroads or fork in the trail while he could still make out the prints. If they could determine a direction, it would allow them to continue their pursuit. Then, quite without warning, all of the tracks stopped.

'What the hell. . . ?' He remembered a lady was present and smothered the profanity. 'Ahem, I mean, something is totally askew.'

Eva came up alongside and looked at him. The poncho she wore was too large for her and her light-weight riding-hat was not intended to withstand a deluge of water. Her hair had been tied back with a ribbon, but it now hung down on to her shoulders; water dripped from her eyelashes and she appeared soaked to the bone.

Rance wished he had saved a hat from one of the three men he'd left in the gully. To her credit, Eva had not said a word in complaint. He suppressed his sympathy for her and got down from his horse. After walking around and checking the muddy trail for a few minutes, he mounted up again.

'They turned around,' he informed her. 'This was a false trail. Our boys figured the rain would wash away the tracks long before anyone got this far. We've been following three or four horses, but now the riders have doubled back.' Rance frowned in thought. 'I've a feeling we were going the right way when we were in pursuit of your brother. He was headed east when we were ambushed.'

'What is east of here?'

'It's the town I mentioned, Wayward.'

'I've been living in Dry Creek for several months and never heard of it.'

'No surprise there. It was nothing more than a trading post and rest stop for the stagecoach for a number of years before it expanded into a town. I rode through there a couple years ago to visit an old army pal of mine. He started up a blacksmith's and livery stable there. With a couple working mines and some ranches in the area, it has prompted the building and growth of the settlement.'

'What do we do now?'

'As we didn't catch up with the men we were following it seems they didn't stop to wait for their three pals. I'm guessing they headed for a designated meeting place, most probably Wayward.'

'If they are mixed in with a lot of townsmen, travelers and miners, how will we know them?' Eva asked. 'Unless I hear the voice of the one man who spoke I won't recognize any of the attackers.'

'They will have our horses,' Rance reminded her. 'I'll speak to my friend at the livery and see what he knows. We find the horses, we find the men we're looking for.'

'Then, we are going to Wayward to try and catch the killers?'

'The only thing you're going to catch in this rain is

pneumonia. We'll head back to the cabin, dry off and wait out the storm.'

'Isn't that dangerous?' she worried. 'I mean, what if they come to check on Corwin and me?'

'If they were going to visit the cabin we'd have run into them. I believe we'll be safe for a few hours.'

'Then what?'

'With three of their men missing they will be on alert for anyone on their back trail. It means we will have to approach Wayward carefully.'

Eva's teeth were beginning to chatter. 'G-getting out of the c-cold, wet weather sounds like a good idea. This horse will be getting spooked when my knees start knocking together.'

The office door opened and Joe entered the room. He saw Yancy at his desk and closed the door behind him. Two strides put him across from his partner.

'It's just as we feared,' he told Yancy with a long face. 'All three of our men are dead. Junior and the boys grabbed the Wells, Fargo agent. He was on his way back to Dry Creek.'

'Just him?'

Joe took a moment to explain everything Junior had told him, then added how his younger brother had shot Hurst and left his body to rot with their three men in the gully. He finished by telling him that the woman and Fayne were still searching for the rest of the gang.

'Of all the stupid blunders!' Yancy slammed his fist on the desktop. 'This is exactly what I didn't want.'

'I took a close look at Fayne's rig a few minutes ago.

There was a bullet lodged in the pommel, right below the saddle horn. That's what saved him from one of the slugs. The other bullet obviously didn't do much damage. The way he was knocked from his horse and tumbled down that hillside – hell, I figured he was done for.'

'You should have had someone check the body right then.'

Joe ducked his head and sighed. 'Yeah, I messed up and three of our boys paid the price.'

Yancy knew swearing and apportioning blame did little good. What was done was past. He had to take the next step and make sure nothing else went wrong.

'I ordered Chuck to double the guard and warn the help to be on the lookout for Fayne. If he or the girl shows up we'll hear about it right away.'

'They will be sure to notice the lady,' Joe said with a grin. 'It was mighty tempting to taste that gal's charms. She's something special.'

'Yes, she's a special problem,' Yancy said. 'We can't kill a woman.'

'Red Dog ain't squeamish.'

Yancy executed a negative twitch. 'No!' he declared adamantly. 'I told you what we would do, when and if it becomes necessary. Our first concern is Fayne; he's more deadly than the plague. If that man-hunter shows his face in Wayward, I want him dead.' He glared at Joe. 'Dead. Not wounded, not running around killing more of our incompetent men, but dead.'

'I'll have a man keep watch down both the east and west trail,' Joe said. 'If those two come riding this direction, we'll know about it and be ready.'

'Good. I don't want to be caught unaware.'

Joe pivoted about to leave. 'I'll take care of everything, boss.'

Yancy waited until Joe was gone before putting fingers to his temples and rubbing the dull ache in his head. Ransom Fayne had not only survived the ambush, he had killed three of his men. He had to wonder how Corwin had coerced the notorious bounty hunter into getting involved. His contact in Dry Creek informed him that no reward had been posted for Nelson Parrish. The agent had been trying to salvage his job and had kept the news of the robbery quiet. So what inducement did Corwin use to obtain the services of the most feared tracker and hunter in the country?

He expelled a deep breath and removed a bottle of brandy. After pouring a small amount in a glass, he took a sip and closed his eyes. Too bad about Corwin Hurst. His attempt to save face and his position had cost him his life. Joe's worthless, bloodthirsty brother had killed him. It was probably for the best. If Hurst had returned to Dry Creek he would have told the sheriff where the ambush had occurred. It might have put the law on their trail and eventually led them to Wayward. With his death, no one was the wiser.

As for the bounty hunter, if Fayne should somehow track his men back to town, death would be his singular reward. The girl was a problem he hadn't counted on dealing with. But she had made her choice and sealed her fate by joining up with a bounty hunter. Yancy had sweated blood to get what he wanted and he would do whatever it took to keep it.

*

The rain slackened to a steady drizzle. Once at the cabin Rance started a fire and left Eva inside. He put the two horses in the old miners' cave, stripped off their gear and tethered them to a rock. Then he scouted around and pulled some leafy shrubs and what grass he could find for fodder. For water, he had let them drink from a reasonably deep puddle before putting them away.

One of the dead trio's saddle-bags had a tin of beans and a few strips of jerky. The other man had carried tobacco and a flask of whiskey. Rance took the liquor with him along with the food and went to the shack.

'Comin' in,' he announced, opening the door slowly.

'It's all right,' Eva answered back. 'I'm decent.'

Rance entered to find a candle burning on the rickety old table. Between it and the light from the fire Eva was clearly visible. He saw she was sitting on an old deer skin next to the fire, trying to warm her hands. She had a blanket wrapped about her and her clothes were draped over a cord a few feet from the fireplace. Likely it was the rope that had been used to bind her and Corwin.

'Ought to warm up in here pretty soon,' he said, pushing the door closed behind him. 'I see you found a dry blanket.'

'It w-was the cover on the m-makeshift bed,' Eva said, her teeth clicking together from her being both wet and cold. 'I had to do b-battle with a couple of perturbed mice, but I convinced them I was serious about taking it. They ch-chose to preserve their lives and escaped through a hole in the wall.'

'You're freezing,' Rance said, shrugging out of the poncho. 'Get closer to the fire.'

'It . . . it doesn't help,' she replied, visibly trembling.

'Here.' Rance offered her the flask of whiskey. 'Take a couple sips of this rotgut.'

He removed his jacket while Eva took a swallow of the hard liquor. She coughed and it caused her eyes to water.

'Gads,' she wheezed. 'How can anyone drink this stuff?'

'It will help to warm your innards,' Rance said. Then he set the bottle aside and sat down behind her, astraddle, with a leg to either side. Gently, so as not to alarm her, he put his arms around her and pulled her back against his chest. Once she had relaxed in his embrace he began to rub her arms and shoulders through the blanket with his hands, working to promote enough friction to generate heat.

It took fifteen minutes of massage and holding her tight before Eva stopped quivering. Finally, Rance ceased the kneading with his hands and simply encircled her with his arms. They remained that way for a short while, until her body began to radiate heat. What happened next left Rance dumbfounded and posed like a statue. Eva's head sagged forward and he realized she had nodded off.

Some thirty minutes passed before Eva abruptly came awake. She jerked up to a sitting position and hastily pulled the blanket up to cover her very inviting neck. Rance unlaced his arms and moved stiffly round to sit beside her. His body oozed with a subtle appreciation for relaxing the muscles in his back and shoulders.

Eva's first effort to get her voice working managed only a muffled squeak of embarrassment. She groaned at the awkward situation.

'I can't believe I actually went to sleep.'

'It's the normal thing to do,' Rance said gently. 'Awake all night, then wet and freezing cold for several hours. It takes a lot out of a person. Getting warm is like after eating a big meal . . . makes a body want to sleep for a spell.'

'I think the whiskey had something to do with it,' she retorted. 'It's . . . absurd, an insult to you. I'm sorry.'

'Don't apologize for the best half-hour of my life,' he chided her. 'You needed a few minutes rest and I have a memory that will last me all my born days.'

Eva turned her head, cast a sidelong look at him, and managed a slight smile. 'Corwin would have a cow, if he were to walk in on us about now.'

'Yep,' Rance responded wryly. 'Reckon it would put an end to the courtship he has been having with you in his head.'

She laughed at the notion. 'The poor man. He doesn't possess enough humility to imagine how I've been able to resist his charms these past weeks.'

'The gent has a lot to offer – good job, a high social position in town, earning a very good wage. Not to mention that he isn't the homeliest man around.'

'Perhaps, but I sometimes felt he chose me because of my looks, not because he actually had a fondness for me,' she suggested. 'His interest in me grew the more I continued to spurn his advances. I believe his main desire was to prove he could have anything or anyone he wanted. The main reason I didn't set him straight is because he's my boss. I didn't want to lose my job.'

'If Corwin, with all of his wit and charm, doesn't light your lamp, then what kind of man are you looking for?' Rance inquired.

Eva didn't reply, perhaps considering her response, or thinking his inquiry was too personal.

'I'm sorry.' He let the matter drop. 'That isn't a proper question for a young lady to have to answer ... especially to a rogue like me.'

'A rogue?'

'Bounty hunting is not a respectable profession in most social circles. I've told you how I was forced to kill several times. Can't expect you to think of me as you would an ordinary suitor.'

'That isn't true,' Eva objected. 'I've gotten to know you very well.'

'From our sparkling conversation during our dinners together?' he teased. 'I hardly said two words to you.'

'Talking is only a small part of communicating,' Eva contended. 'You are considerate, polite and the most perfect gentleman I've ever met.'

Rance was sucker-punched by the woman's flattery. While his brain tried to determine if she was serious, he rubbed the stubble on his chin.

'I suppose I'd make a good watchdog, if that's what you mean by being a gentleman.'

'That being the case, I shouldn't have to pay for your company on this trip,' Eva teased. 'I should only have to pat you on the head on occasion.'

'A considerate dog-owner feeds their pet at least once

a day, too.'

She laughed. 'Speaking of feeding, do we have anything to eat?'

'Not so you need worry about gaining any weight,' he said. He tipped his head at the saddle-bags he had brought in with him. 'We've two air-tights of beans and a little jerky. The ambushers took all of our supplies with our horses. And I don't dare go out and try and find game. A shot would give away our presence here.'

'What about the fire?' she asked. 'Won't the smoke be visible?'

'The storm clouds are practically clinging to the ground, so the smoke can't be seen for any distance. If anyone had got close enough to smell it they would already be on their way here.'

'How come you stayed so warm?' Eva asked. 'Your poncho couldn't have kept you completely dry.'

'I've grown used to being out in the weather. You, being an intelligent woman, probably try to stay out of the cold and the rain.'

Eva gave him a perplexed look. 'It's odd those three men were only carrying a couple cans of beans, isn't it? Our saddle-bags were stuffed completely full. How come the three dead attackers weren't carrying more food or spare clothing? What does it mean?'

'You're very astute for a greenhorn bounty hunter.' Rance praised her deduction. 'It means our ambushers were never more than a day's ride from their hideout.'

'You mean Wayward,' she concluded.

'It is the logical place. No law closer than Dry Creek and it is within eight or ten hours of all three stagecoach hold-ups. I'd say our gang is holed up at or staying very near Wayward.'

Eva looked around. 'With all of the accumulated dust in this place, this certainly wasn't being used as their hideout. No one had spent the night here before Corwin and I did, not for a long time.'

'I didn't get a chance to tell you how sorry I am that your brother was killed.'

A sadness clouded her face. 'Nelly and I were never very close. In fact, he was quite upset when I arrived in Dry Creek and announced I was going to be living there.'

'I thought he got you the job with Wells, Fargo?'

'Corwin gave me the job,' she corrected. 'I stopped by to see Nelly and Corwin asked me about my education. When he learned I was good with numbers and had been doing my father's bookkeeping, he hired me to do the same for Wells, Fargo. I did the nightly audits and would sometimes help during the day. It didn't pay a lot, but it was enough to cover my room and board.'

'Wasn't your father unhappy about both of you leaving him?'

'Father is first and foremost a businessman. Nothing ever got in the way of his business, not my mother or us kids. When Mom died he seemed to withdraw into his work even more than he had before. We seldom saw him except at the mercantile. He hounded Nelly to take on more responsibility and work harder at the business, while I became little more than his servant.' She appeared to reflect on the situation before continuing. 'It fell to me to maintain the house, do the chores, the laundry, the cooking, everything. I would rise early and fix breakfast, work until lunchtime and then take a prepared meal to Father. Then I would hurry back home and do more chores until I started the evening meal. Most nights he brought his account records home for me to check or make entries. I would tally his earnings and count inventory . . . all for no pay. It only got worse when Nelly left, as I had to help at the store too. I had no time or money for myself and no future.'

'You could have gotten married,' Rance suggested.

An odd look passed over Eva's face, as if a hitherto unthinkable notion had occurred to her. She smothered the expression quickly and confessed, 'I never met the right man.'

'So you packed up and left,' Rance finished her story. 'I'm surprised your father sent you the money to keep Wells, Fargo running.'

'It wasn't out of the kindness of his heart.' Her voice was crisp. 'I'm sure Father loathes the idea of Nelly being labeled a bandit and thief. It would reflect badly on him and his business.'

'I see.'

'What about you?' Eva asked, turning the conversation to his life story.

'It's about as I told you. I went to war with several of my friends. None of us believed slavery was right, but we thought that each state should have the right to determine how they would put an end to it. Seemed simple enough – just convert the slaves to sharecroppers or ordinary laborers. If they had been given the freedom to choose their jobs, live where they wanted, and were paid

71

the same as other working men or women, there would
be no need to fight a war.'

'Unfortunately, that didn't happen.'

'No,' Rance said. 'We ended up killing our own
kinfolk, with hundreds of thousands of men dying from
bullets, disease and exposure – nearly destroyed the
entire country.' He shrugged. 'I returned to find our
place had been burned to the ground and my family was
dead. Next, I learned the girl who had promised to wait
for me was married, with one child at her feet and
another on the way. Her husband was a banker's son, a
fellow who had conveniently been overlooked when it
came to conscription.'

'So your heart turned to ice and you decided to make
a living hunting outlaws.'

The words were spoken without censure, but Rance
didn't want Eva thinking of him as cold, callous or
unfeeling.

'In reality,' he replied, 'I went after the three men
responsible for the murder of my family. It happened
that there was a price on their heads. Mad Dog Stokley
and his two brothers had been robbing and looting all
during the war. Killing my family had just been a lark, a
fabricated retaliation for Lawrence, Kansas, when they
were drunk and bored.'

'What horrible men!'

'They put up a fight rather than surrender,' he said.
'When I turned their bodies over to the law in Kansas
City a judge not only got me the reward money due on
them, but gave me handbills on two more. One of those
was an ex-Confederate, but it made no difference to me.

The war was over and a crime was a crime.' He let the narrative die, remembering his anger and rage during those first couple years. He could have easily become a hardhearted killing machine.

'Then,' he continued solemnly, 'I was sent after and caught up with a man who had killed a gent in self-defense. The bounty on him was higher than it should have been and I wondered why. Turns out the fellow he killed was related to a big-city mayor. The mayor had insisted on me being hired to run him to ground because he figured I would bring in his dead body. Instead, he went to trial and an impartial jury trial set him free.'

'So it would have been a revenge killing for the mayor,' Eva deduced.

'That's when I started looking at the job in a different way. Rumor spread that I killed most every man I ever went after,' he said. 'I didn't mind the reputation, because it came in handy. Three of the last four men I captured never put up a fight. One actually came and found me so he could turn himself in.'

'They didn't think they had any chance against you,' Eva mused. 'So the ones who weren't going to hang for their crimes surrendered.'

'In truth, I've only had to kill five of the dozen or so men I've turned in for bounties. The ones who fought and died would have hanged for their crimes, so they had nothing to lose.'

'Why did you decide to help me?' she asked. 'I mean, you seem to have plenty of money.'

'I told you, Wells, Fargo contacted me and asked if I

would look into the robberies. You are probably aware that they offer a hefty bounty for any bandit who hits one of their coaches?'

'Yes.'

'Well, they advanced me five hundred dollars to try and find out if there was an inside man.' He uttered a half-laugh. 'They first attempted to hire a Pinkerton Eye for the job, but they were unable to get a detective over here for several months.'

'That doesn't answer the question as to why you came with Corwin and me.'

Rance circled the wagons in his brain defensively. 'Because I knew you were going to go looking even if I turned you down.'

'But there isn't anyone around as good as you at tracking. I might have never found Nelly's trail.'

'I believe someone was watching Dry Creek,' Rance said.

Eva recalled what the man with the deep voice had said. 'Yes, the men who ambushed us knew the three of us were trying to find my brother.'

'So it didn't matter who you hired. If your guide happened to guess right the ambushers would have been waiting. With me along, I was their prime target. They knew you and Corwin were no real threat to them.'

'OK,' Eva acknowledged. 'You felt allowing me to come along was a way to guard my safety? Is that it?'

'Something like that.'

She studied him with an intense scrutiny. 'Is that the only reason?'

'I don't know.' Rance grinned, trying to bluff his way

without giving an honest answer. 'Maybe I hoped I would end up with you in front of a cozy fireplace, with you wearing nothing but a blanket.'

Her furrowed brow revealed she didn't accept that response. 'You still haven't told me why, Rance.'

A thousand things went through his head, but not one of them made sense. He hated the turmoil that roiled within his chest. This woman was downright unsettling to his nerves, his self-control and even his promise never to get involved with another woman.

'Eva,' he answered after a strained silence, 'I know this isn't the answer you're looking for, but I don't seem to be able to say no to you.'

'That's ridiculous.'

'Yeah, well, so is us being here together, searching for a gang of bandits.' He gazed directly into her bright, ebony-colored eyes, enjoying the subtle intimacy. 'I carried the ache and disappointment from a woman I cared about inside of me for two years. It wasn't until you asked to sit at my table that I was able to put that girl out of my head.'

Eva's eyes widened at his confession. 'You mean to say you are – what – smitten with me?'

'Look in a mirror sometime,' he retorted. 'What man in his right mind wouldn't be?'

That was the end of the inquisition. Eva's lids veiled her eyes and she lowered her head. A crimson flush washed up her cheeks and she appeared at a loss for words.

Way to go, Rance. He cussed his mishandling of what could have been a tender moment between him and a beautiful, desirable young lady. *You've all the tact of a rampaging bull.*

When Eva spoke again it was yonder and dale away from anything remotely romantic. 'Do you have some way to open a can of beans?'

'Uh, yeah,' Rance told her. 'I can use my knife. I imagine you're about starved.'

'We share equally,' she insisted. 'You have to keep up your strength.'

'Yeah, right,' he muttered. *Otherwise, I might fall on my backside when I try and kick myself for telling the truth.*

CHAPTER FIVE

John Kegan sat on a bench in front of his cabin with a lightweight hammer, waiting for the next pesky crow or magpie to come snooping around the dying remnants of his well-tended garden. For two months since giving up his livery he had done nothing more than plant the vegetables in the patch alongside the house. He might have laughed had anyone else called his run-down shanty a house. A single room, cot, rough-hewn table and a lone chair. Even his cook stove was too small for heating the tiny hovel. With winter coming on, he would have to figure a way to keep from freezing.

'Don't turn that lethal-looking weapon on me, pard'-nah.' A drawling voice startled him. 'I don't cotton to unnecessary violence.'

John rose to his feet and spotted Rance. He set the hammer down on the bench as a wide smile spread across his lips. 'Why, bless my aching corns! Ransom Fayne, you lop-eared coyote!'

'You still tossing hammers around instead of forking over the price of a bullet or two?'

'Where's the sport in shooting a defenseless bird?'
John laughed. 'Besides, you remember how much
money and free drinks I won for us with my hammers,
don't you?'

'Yeah, but trying to hit a crow? Those little buggers
are quick.'

'I ain't hit one yet, but a few of them have left evi-
dence behind of what they ate last when I got too close.'

'Scaring them away is probably as good as hitting
them,' Rance observed.

The two men shook hands and John opened the door
to his cabin. 'Come on in, old buddy. I got some corn
liquor that's all of a week old. Ought to be aged 'bout as
sweet as that gal I was sparkin' at Victorville.'

Following him inside, Rance remarked, 'You no-
account reprobate. That woman was old enough to be
your mother.'

'Correct,' John retorted with a grin. 'A more mature
wine is always the sweetest.'

Rance became grave. 'I went through all of the
trouble to sneak into Wayward – walked a good half-mile
through the hills to get there – only to find out you sold
your livery stable. What gives?'

'Sold, says you.' John sneered the words. 'It was stolen
from me.'

'What happened?'

John poured a little snake venom into the only two tin
cups he owned and handed one to Rance. He stepped
over and rested his haunch on the edge of his cot, allowing Rance the single chair.

'New outfit come to town a while back,' he said. He

paused to take a sip of liquor before continuing: 'They commenced to building a whopping big casino at the far end of town. But that wasn't enough for them fellers. One of the top dogs named Joe Marcone walked in one day and handed me three hundred dollars. Said they were buying me out.'

'And you let them? Just like that?'

'Not quite. We bantered back and forth for some time, but it was a stacked deck, pard. If I didn't sell, they were going to open a blacksmith's and stable right across the street. He claimed they would undercut my prices until I went broke. Marcone then informed me they had already underbid my contract with the stage line, so there went a big chunk of my business. I did finally get them to up the price to four hundred, thanks to owning a rental buggy and couple of good horses. Thing is, I seen how much they were spending on the saloon, so I knew I could never outlast them. I was barely getting by before they arrived.'

'What are you doing here in this rickety old shanty?' Rance questioned him. 'Why not move to another town and start over?'

'I aim to, but not until spring. I ain't fond of freezing in the winter while trying to build up a new business.'

Rance took a sip of the home-made brew and coughed. 'Hot damn, John! That stuff is strong enough to melt the wheels off a railroad car.'

'Takes getting used to, youngster.'

'You drink much of this lamp oil and you won't live till spring.'

John snorted disdainfully. 'You never was much of a drinking man.'

Rance placed his cup on the table, unwilling to take a second sip, and returned to business. 'So these guys showed up two or three months ago, huh?'

'Yep, two men runnin' the show and maybe seven or eight flunkies. The main honcho is some feller named Yancy Bodean, but I've only seen him a couple of times. Marcone is the boss on the street. He oversaw most of the work while the saloon was being built.'

When Rance didn't offer an opinion, John eyed him with suspicion. 'What's your interest in all this? You looking to collect a bounty on someone?'

John was eight years Rance's senior, shorter by an inch or two, but his body was muscled and hard from his blacksmith work. Being prematurely gray made him look older and he had a weathered squint, not from the sun but from working over a hot forge, which seared a man's face and arms from the constant heat. Yancy had spent the last two years of the war sharing a tent with the man. John could build 'most anything and was the best man with horses he had ever seen. Rance filled him in on the details of his mission and waited for him to digest the situation.

'You mean to tell me,' John said, after mulling it over for a moment, 'that there's an incredibly beautiful woman watching your horses, less'n a mile from here?'

'Is that the only part of the story you heard?'

John waved his hand to brush off Rance's concern. 'Hell, man, I only listen to what's important. Getting killed comes in a distant second to cozying up to or sweet-talking a lovely lady.'

'How about being outnumbered fifteen to one?'

He snorted. 'Cutting me in on your woes just chopped the number in half. Now it's only eight for you and seven for me.'

'I didn't look you up to get you killed, John.'

'Why else would you be here?' John riposted. 'I know the town, I know most of Bodean's men, and I would risk spilling a little blood to get my livery back . . . preferably not my blood.'

'We can't be a hundred per cent certain the bandits and kidnappers are there . . . or even who they are,' Rance told him. 'The girl only heard one man speak, but she claims she would recognize his voice.'

'From what you've told me, the timing matches up with the hold-ups you mentioned. Building the saloon started about the time Wells, Fargo lost their first shipment of money.'

'Proves nothing if Eva doesn't recognize someone or we don't get a confession.'

'I'll go in and poke around some,' John offered. 'Maybe I can get someone to talk.'

'You'll get yourself strung up from the nearest tree,' Rance disapproved. 'There's other ways to get proof.'

'What kind of proof would that be?'

'The second coach robbery consisted of more than money. There was some jewelry being transported to a storekeeper in Carson City. A couple diamonds, a ruby and several strings of fine gold. It might be difficult to sell stuff like that without raising some questions.'

'You think Bodean might have those items tucked away inside the saloon?' John suggested.

'It isn't something he would have put in a bank,'

81

Rance replied. 'And you did say he spent a lot of money on his casino?'

John nodded. 'It's a first-class place.' He rubbed his hairy chin with the back of his hand. 'I recall a freight wagon that come to town one day, carrying a big crate. Took six strong men to cart it up the saloon stairs, and I heard one of those guys complain the box must have weighed eight hundred pounds.' He winked. 'Bodean has himself a safe.'

'Any idea if Bodean trusts anyone enough for them to have the combination?'

'Maybe Marcone, but I don't really know. They've only been open for business for a coupla weeks. With them stealing my livery, I ain't never wanted to cross their threshold. One carpenter did tell me there are a fair number of rooms upstairs. I reckon that's for the girls and probably Marcone and Bodean. I know the floor manager has a room out back. They also have a bunkhouse of sorts for the guards. Like I said, Bodean went first class on everything.'

'With that many people around it would be hard to get into his safe.'

'There's also guards on duty round the clock,' John advised.

Rance pondered a few ideas. 'Without a way to take a peek into the man's safe, our best bet is to find a way for Miss Parrish to overhear a couple of Bodean's men. If Marcone is his partner or second in command, there's a good chance he is the man we want.'

'Marcone does have a voice like a growling dog,' John mused.

'You said he's the one who bought your livery?'

'Stole it,' John corrected. Then, with a sneer of contempt, 'Put his worthless brother in to run the place. Junior Marcone has a hostler to handle the horses, so he just sits around either chawing on or smoking tobacca. Man don't work a lick.'

'If I could get the girl into town, close enough to overhear a conversation, do you think you could get the elder Marcone to talk to you?'

'What about?'

'Maybe you could say you wanted to buy back one of the horses he bought from you. Or you might have left some tools behind. After all, you'll need those tools when you start up a new business.'

'I did leave my work hammers, tongs and chisels,' John confessed. 'And it takes a year or more to break in a hammer properly.' He harrumphed. 'Junior is such a lame excuse for a blacksmith, he wouldn't know pincer tongs from a leather punch.'

'That might work, John, so long as you could get into the discussion where the lady can overhear Marcone's voice.'

'I could probably get him to the livery. Mayhaps you and the gal could hide out in the loft or one of the stalls, close enough to listen in. The forge is at the front of the barn just beyond the stable. If we did it after dark, you two could slip right in close. Ought to be easy enough to overhear our dickering over a price for my tools.'

'We'll do it tonight,' Rance decided. 'Do we need to worry about anyone coming to visit you?'

John chuckled. 'I ain't been the best of company since

I lost my business. You and the woman can stay here till it's time to go to town. I'll even rustle you up something to eat while you go fetch her.'

Rance shook John's hand again. 'I knew I could count on you.'

'Yeah,' John said. 'It's been some time since you last tried to get me kilt.'

'I seem to remember you got us both into a few scrapes when we were fighting the Yanks, too.'

John grinned. 'We always got out alive.' Then, speaking half-seriously, 'Reckon we'll try and have the same outcome this go-round.'

Joe Marcone entered the casino and experienced an immediate satisfaction. The place was full of miners and even a few soldiers from a supply train. They had ridden twenty miles to spend their money at the newest, biggest, most fancy saloon within a hundred miles. Belle was singing a tune and flashing a smile at the customers. She was a little past her prime, but she could still belt out a melody. The other girls were visiting tables and mingling with customers.

Spotting a shadow at the upstairs office, Joe knew Yancy was in his usual place. When there was but a single lamp burning in the room it was dark enough to make it nearly impossible to see the man standing behind his window. Joe threaded his way through the crowd and went up the guarded stairway. He and Yancy were partners, but he still showed the courtesy of knocking at the door. After all, Yancy was the brains behind this venture.

'Come in, Joe,' Yancy called from the other side.

Joe went inside and joined Yancy at the window, from where he was able to look over the crowded main floor. As his partner didn't offer to start the conversation, he gave him the latest news.

'Red Dog rode out and looked for sign on the main trail this morning. He didn't find any tracks of Fayne and the woman, but the rain pretty much washed the roadway clean.'

'So we can't assume they followed the false trail and continued to Reno,' Yancy reasoned. 'No word from our pigeon in Dry Creek?'

'Nothing yet,' Joe replied. 'Corwin told us the man he left in charge was not supposed to report the robbery for two weeks. We've plenty of time before anyone contacts Wells, Fargo.'

'I doubt anyone will ever find Corwin's body, not if that gully is as deep as you claim.'

'There's an outside chance the rain could have washed his or one of the other bodies down the mountain somewhere,' Joe acknowledged. 'But if that happened it would be nearly impossible to identify the corpse.'

Yancy rubbed his hands together thoughtfully and moved to other concerns. 'What do you think Fayne will do once he discovers we didn't go to Reno?'

'My guess, he will return the woman to Dry Creek. No way he would spend several days trying to pick up a cold trail with a female along.' Joe grunted his confidence. 'Besides, the man ain't got a clue as to where to start looking and don't have a description of any of us. We all had masks on when we took the girl and Corwin prisoners, and we covered their heads with hoods. Only time I let the girl take a look was to see the body at the bottom of that old mineshaft, and I made darn sure her eyes didn't wander nowhere else.'

Yancy pondered the options and had to agree. Fayne was wandering about in an underground maze without light of any kind . . . no clue to their whereabouts, no idea as to their numbers, and not one eyewitness who had ever seen their faces.

'All the same,' he told Joe, 'let's keep the men alert and posted on the trail. If Fayne happens to come looking this way we'll be alerted ahead of time. He has no reason to suspect anyone here in Wayward.'

'Sure 'nuff,' Joe agreed. 'If he comes snooping, he'll find absolutely nothing. Then if he doesn't move on . . .' He drew a line across his throat to demonstrate the end of Ransom Fayne.

Yancy looked back down to the floor. 'Uh-oh. Chuck just pointed a finger up our way. Someone must want to talk to one of us.'

Joe stared down and spotted the man Yancy was talking about. 'It's Kegan, the ex-blacksmith. Wonder what he wants?'

'Mebbe should have kept him on for a bit. Your brother can't weld two tin cans together.'

'Had to give Junior a job somewhere, boss,' Joe rationalized. 'He never could play cards worth a hoot and takes five minutes to get his gun out of its holster. Can't even run a roulette wheel. I figure he can at least tend horses.'

'Go take care of whatever it is Kegan wants. One of

the boys said he was going to leave town in the spring and start a business in a new location.'

'Right,' Joe said. 'I'll deal with him.'

John stopped questioning Chuck when he saw Marcone coming down the stairs. 'Reckon we was being spied upon from up above,' he said to the floor manager.

'Mr Bodean is usually watching,' Chuck replied. 'I hope Marcone can make things right concerning your tools.'

John thanked him and waited for Marcone to arrive. There was no animosity in the man's expression, just a mild irritation.

'What's going on, Kegan?' he asked. 'Didn't you swear to never set foot in our place?'

'I'm about to go nutty in that tiny cabin of mine. I reckon I ought to be moving on,' John explained. 'Reason I'm here, it occurred to me that your brother took over my place with most of my tools. There are a few things I left behind that can't easily be replaced.'

'Such as?'

'It takes a good blacksmith – and I ain't talking about no one like that fumble-fisted brother of yours,' he clarified. 'Anyhow, it takes a year and sometimes longer to get a hammer honed to just the right feel. Junior wouldn't know a good hammer from a hot poker, so I'm asking you to let me pick up a few of the tools I left behind. They won't do him any good, 'cause he ain't no black-smith.'

Joe pondered on the problem for a moment. 'How many tools are we talking about?'

'A couple of my favorite hammers, pincers and chisels mainly,' John said. 'I would also like a punch or two and maybe another pair of tongs. Shouldn't be more than eight or ten items.'

'I'll tell my brother when I see him.'

'I'd be right appreciative if you'd walk over with me right now, so I won't have to make a second trip, should Junior give me grief. Like I said, I've decided not to sit out the winter. There's a few places down Arizona way that don't get any snow or real cold weather. I thought I might mosey down and have a look-see soon as I get a few things together.'

Joe removed his pocket watch and heaved a sigh of resignation. 'All right. Let's go over to the livery before Junior turns the place over to the night hostler, and get this over with.'

'Thanks a lot, Mr Marcone,' John said. 'I should've mentioned it when you bought the place, but I was kinda out of sorts over losing it.' He shrugged. 'You know how it is.'

'Yeah,' Joe replied, not the least interested. 'So let's not stand here jawing. I got other things to do.'

Rance avoided the main trails and led Eva through the darkness on foot. It was a cool night so they both wore jackets. It was a plus that their coats were both brown in colour, as it provided additional concealment in the darkness. They entered Wayward from the less populated side of town, below the livery's horse corral. He had her stay hidden until he moved up to calm the animals. He spoke softly to them so they wouldn't spook and Eva came forward at his wave. She stopped suddenly and pointed.

'That's the horse you rented for me!' she exclaimed in a hushed voice.

'All three are here,' Rance acknowledged. 'Means those ambushers either traded our horses or they are in town. We still need to figure out which.'

'I understand,' she said. 'To start asking people questions would give us away.'

'Let's go ahead with the plan.'

Eva nodded her accord and they carefully made their way to the rear entrance to the barn. The door was ajar enough for Rance to peek inside. The interior was dark except at the very front of the building, where the blacksmith tools and forge were located. He eased the door open wide enough for the two of them to enter and they slipped inside.

The problem was to get Eva close enough to hear Marcone's voice loud and clear. Rance and Eva traversed the stable slowly and quietly, mindful not to startle the couple horses in the stalls. The hayloft was to the front of the structure, but the way up there was blocked. The only access ladder stood next to where the liveryman was sitting on a work stool. He had some reading material in his hands, his feet were propped up on an old wagon wheel. A lamp hanging from a nail on the wall gave off light from over the back of his shoulder.

'This is too far away,' Eva whispered nervously. They had reached the last stall and stopped at a stack of grain-filled gunnysacks. 'Your friend said he would only be able to enter the front as far as the work bench and forge.'

The evening shadows hid them where they were, but they needed to move closer. Even as Rance mulled over how to find a better spot, Marcone and John came walking down the street. Eva panicked at possibly missing their chance. Before Rance could stop her she darted forward to the forge and dropped to her knees, hiding behind the brick foundation of the open hearth. By hunkering down, she was hidden from the doorway and was out of sight, unless Marcone or the man with the magazine walked beyond the work area far enough to see her.

Rance held his breath, unable to do anything but watch. There wasn't enough hiding-space for him to join Eva, so he could only wait in the darkness. He worried about the rear door being so far away. If spotted, Eva would never make it out. Nevertheless, it was too late to change tactics as John and Marcone had arrived at the barn. The man who had been lounging up front got lazily to his feet.

'Hey, big brother!' he greeted Marcone, ambling over to meet them. 'What are you doing with the old blacksmith?'

'Kegan wants a few of his tools, Junior. We didn't exactly cover all we were buying when I paid him for the livery. He's looking to take about a dozen pieces.'

Eva signaled frantically to Rance. She recognized Joe Marcone as the man who had kidnapped her! He held up a hand, showing he understood, but also telling her to remain where she was. Joe was facing the forge and would surely see her if she moved.

Junior had been chewing tobacco. He paused to spit,

but much of it dribbled down his chin. He quickly wiped with the back of his hand and shrugged. 'Makes no never-mind to me. I can always buy anything I might need.'

'If you ever do any real blacksmith work,' John taunted critically, 'you'll find that you need a hammer that has the right feel. A good hammer has to be properly rounded for pounding hot iron without having the handle slip.'

Junior displayed a cocky smirk. 'If you say so, Kegan.'

'Get the tools you mentioned and let's be done with this,' Joe growled.

John picked up a gunnysack and selected several items: two hammers, a couple chisels, a punch, and one each of the tongs and pincers. He hefted the bag after he finished and turned to face the two men.

'That will have to do,' he said. 'Now, if I have to, I can build or buy me a portable forge. That way I can work while moving around from place to place.'

'Take your stuff and be gone, Kegan.' Marcone was gruff. 'I don't expect to see your ugly puss at the livery again.'

'Shouldn't be a problem,' John answered back. 'Thanks for being civil about this.'

The two Marcone brothers watched the ex-blacksmith as he walked off down the street. Two riders passed by John, both plainly headed to the barn. Rance began to sweat. If the new arrivals decided to put up their horses, Eva would have a heck of a time staying out of sight. Rance put his hand on the butt of his gun, but he couldn't take on four men, not with Eva in the middle of the battle. Plus, one shot would likely bring a dozen more men to the livery. Helpless to do anything else, he backed up a step, moving deeper into the shadows.

Joe turned to his brother and commented, 'We should have kept Kegan working here until you learned the trade.'

'Nothing to learn,' Junior retorted haughtily. 'I ain't looking to be no blacksmith.'

'It's the only decent job I could find for you,' Joe said. 'Would you rather end up working for Lefty as a saloon guard, or pulling duty like Sadler and Topknot, riding patrol for twelve hours at a time? Ask them how much fun that is when they get here to put away their horses for the night. This is a good place to be, out of weather, tending a few horses and mending a wagon or saddle strap once in a while.'

'I'd make more money with my gun.'

'You ain't never going to be a gunman, Junior. I don't aim to see you getting killed because you can't shoot straight.'

Junior came erect. 'I shoot straight enough. I killed that Wells, Fargo agent with a single shot.'

A sudden, involuntary gasp escaped Eva's lips.

The Marcone brothers both heard it. Joe pulled his gun and waved frenetically at the two approaching riders to come running. Junior also had his pistol out and began to move toward the forge. As several men converged on the barn, Eva had no chance for escape.

Rance's single option was to run. He used the shadows, moving quickly and silently until he reached the back door. Even as the men swarmed over Eva's hiding-place, he was out into the night and hurrying away from the building.

The plan had backfired. They had learned Joe Marcone was one of the ambushers, but Eva was their prisoner for the second time. Not yet knowing how many bandits he was pitted against, Rance faced a new task – rescuing Eva.

CHAPTER SIX

Joe barked orders to his men and sent them scurrying. Then, grabbing hold of Eva's wrists, he dragged her along the dirt floor of the livery, out into the open. He released his hold, hovered over her menacingly and bared his teeth like an enraged dog.

'Where's the bounty hunter, you sneaky little she-cat?' Joe snarled the question, his fist raised, poised to strike. 'Where's the guy who killed three of my men? Tell me, or I'll squash your nose all over your pretty face!'

Eva drew back defensively, hands thrown up to ward off a blow. 'He died from his wounds,' she cried, quickly making up an answer.

'Oh, he died.' Joe's voice was filled with sarcasm. 'Don't give me that garbage.'

'It's true,' Eva replied, presenting her most honest look. 'I came to town to find help and borrow a horse, so I could get back home.'

'Why didn't you leave with Hurst?' he fired back.

'Corwin wanted to get back to Dry Creek and his job.' She continued the story-telling. 'He didn't want to stick

94

around and wait until Mr Fayne either recovered or died.'

'She's lying her head off,' Junior sneered. 'That sniveling agent told us Fayne's wound was little more than a scratch. He said you and the bounty hunter were going to follow us to the ends of the earth.'

Eva maintained her bluff. 'I can't be held responsible for what Corwin might have said. He probably didn't want you thinking of him as a coward.'

'Don't trust a word she says,' Junior told his brother. 'Fayne is around here somewhere.'

A man entered the barn before Joe could continue the interrogation. The new arrival gave a negative shake of his head.

'Nothing,' he said. 'We did a quick search around town. If Fayne was here, he slipped away into the hills. Red Dog couldn't find any tracks – too blasted dark.'

'All right, Sadler. Have Lefty warn his people and tell the other boys to stay alert. Fayne is dangerous and smart.'

'Digger, Sal and Needle can vouch for the dangerous part,' Junior chimed in, naming their three dead *compadres*.

Joe put his hands on his hips and issued orders.

'Tell anyone who asks that this gal is wanted for murder and robbery. Fayne is her partner in crime and will likely try to rescue her. No one is to talk to this little ferret without my say-so.'

'Where do we put her?'

'Stick her in the smokehouse. Put two men on the door and another keeping watch from a window or rooftop so no one can sneak up on them.'

'I'll see to everything personally,' Sadler assured him.

'Junior, you go with him and lock up this lying vixen. I'll tell the boss what is going on and see what he wants to do.'

'Only one thing to do,' Junior shot back. 'We give her a quick trial and hang her.'

Joe scowled at him. 'Just this once, you do as you're told.'

The younger Marcone bridled at Joe's slapping him down in front of Sadler. He suppressed the humiliation by jabbing Eva in the ribs with the toe of his boot. She sucked in her breath from the sharp pain, but didn't cry out.

'Get up, woman,' he ordered. 'You want to keep your hair and good looks, you'll do exactly as I say.'

Eva quickly got to her feet. Junior took hold of her arm, his fingers like talons that dug right through her jacket and into her flesh. She wisely masked the discomfort and kept pace when he set off down the street. Sadler waved over another man and the three of them escorted her to a block building a short way from the saloon.

Eva was pushed inside the sturdy structure, which smelled of burnt wood and raw meat. Not a glimmer of light was visible once the door closed. She was left groping in the dark, hoping to not run into any meat hooks that might be hanging down in front of her. When she located a wooden counter, she carefully ran her fingers over the surface until she ascertained its size and that it was clean of debris. Fearful of sharing the floor with snakes or other creepy, crawling creatures in such utter blackness, she opted to snug her jacket about her tightly and stretch out on the tabletop.

Once able to relax, albeit on uncomfortable wooden slabs, she worried what would happen next. She knew Rance was both crafty and deadly in any kind of fight, but the odds were overwhelming. How could he and John ever hope to rescue her, when it seemed the entire town was pitted against them?

If only I hadn't let them hear me, she thought woefully. But she had been completely unprepared for the news about Corwin. He had been captured, possibly tortured, and finally killed. Lawrence, the man running the Wells, Fargo office, would wait until the two weeks were up. Then he would notify the company of what had happened. The owners would have not only to repay her father, but cover the loss of a major payroll theft as well. The one positive thing she could depend upon at the moment was Rance. She had to believe he would find a way to save her. Within the total blackness that consumed everything around her, Eva stared up toward the ceiling and began to pray.

Rance entered John's cabin an hour after Eva had been captured. His friend had coffee perking on the stove, along with a bottle of whiskey sitting on the table.

'Beginning to worry about you,' John greeted him. 'Tell me you didn't go and get your tail twisted in a knot.'

Rance explained about Eva getting too close as he sagged down on the single wobbly chair and rested his elbows on the table. 'When she heard Junior say Corwin was dead . . .' He sighed and poured a little whiskey into his coffee cup. 'There wasn't a thing I could do. Two of Marcone's boys rode up about the time Eva gave away her position and Joe signaled for even more men. It was run or be caught in a gunfight with a half-dozen or more gunmen.'

'That there's a fine kettle of wildcats. Now what?' John wanted to know. 'You think they might hurt the girl in an effort to force her to talk?'

Rance stared at his cup without taking a sip. 'No, I don't.'

'But she knows who they are!' John exclaimed. 'More than that, *where* they are!'

'If they were going to kill her,' Rance reasoned, 'why not do it right away? They let her and Corwin live. If I hadn't killed the three men who came back to check on me, Eva and Corwin would have probably gotten back to Dry Creek safely.'

'Yeah, but them boys *did* kill Corwin.'

'Only after questioning him about me.' Rance continued to think aloud. 'I don't think they want to murder a woman. Especially someone like Eva. Her father has a business in Carson City and probably knows some important people. Eva was also an employee of the Wells, Fargo company. Killing Corwin was one thing, but to slay a woman? A beautiful, well-respected woman?'

'On the flip side of the coin, these fellers have taken root in Wayward; she knows that's where they are, so they can't turn her loose. What does that leave?'

'They'll probably try and use her for bait,' Rance guessed. 'Hold her hostage until I make a move to free her.'

'Makes sense,' John agreed. 'You can bet their first order of business is to have every man Jack they can get scouring the hills for you come daylight. Once you are dead, their identity and location are safe.'

'Except for Eva.'

'Yep. After you're planted in a hole, they have two ways to deal with your girlfriend,' John summarized, 'they either have to kill her or make her disappear.'

'Disappear.' Rance mouthed the word thoughtfully. 'You're right, of course. They have to get rid of her one way or the other.'

John thoughtfully scratched his shaggy head. 'Looks like the smart move is not to let yourself get killed, pard.'

'We need to find out what their intentions are,' Rance suggested. 'I came along a run-off ditch when I left town. Nothing short of a bloodhound will locate my trail. We should be safe for a bit, but how do we find out what they are going to do with Eva?'

'I'll take my pack animal to town,' John suggested. 'I can buy some supplies for my trip and maybe pick up some local gossip. A couple of the old timers don't care for Bodean's new casino and the passel of gunmen working for him.'

'You ask too many questions and it might give away we are working together. If they start to suspect you. . . .'

John held up his hand to stop Rance's warnings or protest. 'This ain't my first dance, old buddy. I know when to kick up my heels and when to sit on the side-lines.'

'What about the two horses out back? They belonged to the men who dry-gulched me.'

'If anyone shows up to ask, I'll say I found them wandering loose.'

Rance hated to think of Eva being a prisoner all night, but it was too risky to venture back to town. She would be well guarded and men with guns would be searching for him most of the night. Their only alternative was to sit it out, wait until morning and see what John could learn.

'I'll move to a secluded position before first light,' he told John. 'If I can find a spot high enough, maybe I can keep an eye on the trail in or out of town.'

'The hill back of this here cabin should do the trick. There's a fair-sized boulder up near the crest. You hunker down behind it and you can see for a mile in either direction.' John brought the coffee pot to the table. 'Just make certain no one sees you up there. Marcone has more men than the two of us can handle at one time.'

'I'll be in position before it gets light,' Rance vowed. He might have added: *because I'm not going to sleep a wink until I get Eva back.*

Yancy stormed around the office, swearing and muttering oaths. He finally stopped and looked at Joe.

'You're sure Corwin told the truth, that the bounty hunter didn't die?'

'Junior said the agent was too scared to lie to them,' Joe answered. 'I reckon he told it straight.'

'No one saw Fayne enter or leave the barn?'

Joe pulled a face. 'Afraid not, boss. Don't know how they done it, but they got into town without anyone seeing them.'

'This is exactly what I didn't want to happen.' Yancy cursed. 'We had the perfect hideout, the perfect place to disappear. You and I were going to make a fortune on this place and sell it before the ore plays out in the mines. We'd then move to San Francisco and open the kind of casino that would keep us rolling in money for the rest of our lives.'

'We can still make that happen,' Joe insisted. 'Two loose ends is all we have to deal with, and the girl is already our prisoner. Fayne can't be far away. I told the people who were curious the story we agreed on concerning our prisoner. Lefty is assigning his guards to join us. Come morning, we will send patrols in every direction. We acted too quick for Fayne to have escaped on a horse. He's got to be close.'

'OK.' Yancy simmered down. 'We know Fayne won't go anywhere without the girl. He let her come with him. Then she stayed with him instead of leaving with Corwin. It would seem those two have developed a relationship of some kind, which fits in with our account about him and the girl.'

'Once we get Fayne, then what?'

'We'll stick to the plan as outlined. You're sure Red Dog knows the right people?'

'He rode with El Gato's Comanchero gang for a year or so before he crossed the border and joined us.' Joe uttered a satisfied grunt. 'Yeah, he can do the job.'

'We have to make sure everything is taken care of.' Yancy mulled over a few ideas. 'If we don't locate Fayne tomorrow, we'll set a trap for him with the lady. I'm betting that big, bad, famous man-hunter will risk his life to get her back. We'll use his fondness for the girl and get rid of him for good.'

'I like the sound of that,' Joe admitted. 'Taking on a deadly gunman like Fayne, we need every advantage possible.'

'Make sure Fayne can't get to the girl. Can't have her being rescued and ruining our plans.'

'I've got that covered, boss,' Joe promised.

'Thanks, Joe,' Yancy said. 'I'm glad that you and I are partners. You are the only man I can trust to get every job done right.'

Joe shook his head. 'Every job except one. That mistake cost us three of our men.'

'That's one time you should have been doing the shooting,' Yancy agreed. 'However, the two who missed ended up paying the price for their failure.'

'Let's hope we find him tomorrow, boss. Knowing how deadly Fayne is, it will be hard to get men to act as bait.'

'We'll offer a bonus – five hundred dollars for each man who volunteers to take the girl to the border.'

Joe's face lit up. 'That sure ought to get enough men to do the job.' He grinned. 'All the same, I won't tell the boys about the bonus unless we fail to find Fayne tomorrow.'

'The same offer stands for the hunt: five hundred to anyone who kills Fayne.'

'That should make the boys a little more eager. Many of them were dreading the chore of searching for a man as deadly as him.'

'Get some rest,' Yancy said. 'You'll need to be up early

to supervise the search.'

'Yeah, boss. I'll take care of it.'

Yancy frowned. 'Joe, you don't have to keep calling me boss. We're equal partners in this venture.'

Joe laughed. 'I do that so the boys will respect you.' Then, with a wink, 'And I can also tell them I have no choice when a dirty job comes along. I blame it on you.'

A rare smile came to Yancy's face. 'I see. You make me out to be the tyrant, while you play along as one of the sycophants.'

'Syco-what?'

'It means something like a yes-man, Joe.'

'Funny-sounding word, but using it makes you sound a whole lot smarter than the rest of us.'

'Pretentious is another of those words,' Yancy said. 'But that pertains to me.'

Joe laughed again. 'Whatever you say, boss.'

It was a long, restless night on a cold, hard table. Eva didn't realize it was morning until the door opened. The light of day nearly blinded her, forcing her to shield her eyes from the brightness.

'Brought you breakfast.' A man wearing a fashionable bowler hat spoke up. 'I also have a jug of water and a couple candles.'

'You're keeping me in here?' Eva inquired hesitantly.

'Only until tomorrow morning. I'm not sure what is planned, but Mr Bodean ordered me to see to your needs.'

'Mr Bodean?'

'He and Marcone pretty much own the town, ma'am.

I'm Chuck Lefever, the floor manager at their casino.'

Eva blinked several times and was finally able to see the man. He wore a clean suit and was clean-shaven other than for a thick mustache. He put the dish of food and other items on the table next to her.

'I'll see you get a couple blankets,' Chuck offered, looking around. 'Didn't know they had stuck you in here with nothing but the light coat you're wearing.'

'Thank you,' Eva said.

The man removed a match, struck it, and lit one of the candles. He upended it, using a bit of the wax for a base, then stuck the candle on a narrow counter that looked like a place to store tools and knives. It was currently empty of anything but dust.

'I'll trust you aren't reckless enough to try and set fire to the place,' Chuck said. 'This smoke shack is both sod and wood. You would likely suffocate from the smoke long before it burned enough to be noticed from the outside. Plus, the guards have orders not to open the door for anything or anyone but me.'

'I am not yet ready to commit suicide,' she announced.

'Good,' he said. 'I'll be back with blankets about lunchtime.' He waited, but she said nothing. 'OK then. You might as well make yourself comfortable. This place is under heavy guard. No one will be coming for you, not unless they are in a hurry to meet their Maker.'

'Thank you for your kindness,' she said.

Chuck tipped his bowler hat and went out the door. Once it was securely closed Eva picked up the jug and took a drink. It was awkward not having a glass, but satisfying none the less. The water was cool and soothed her parched throat. She picked at the food, but she didn't have much of an appetite. Uncertainty about her future and worrying about Rance replaced hunger pangs with fear and apprehension.

Rance had proved he was capable. His returning from the first deadly ambush with a mere scratch was amazing in itself, but he had also dispatched three of the ambushers in the process. When he had talked about his reputation being overblown she had pretty much agreed with him. But now, facing such incredible odds, she hoped every word was true. She needed a hero, a bedtime-story knight in shining armor, one who could defeat an army single-handed.

She almost smiled at the thought. He wasn't alone. He had his friend, the ex-blacksmith. She hoped with all of her heart the two of them would be enough.

CHAPTER SEVEN

John had been correct about the lookout point. At daylight, from the cover of a huge boulder near the summit of one of the highest hills around, Rance was able to see the main trail in and out of town, several of the major buildings, and the terrain on three sides of the region for a goodly distance. Unlike most obvious perches, the stone face melded into the side of the slope, making it unobtrusive and adequately concealing the notch from where he could keep his vigil.

Having lost his own equipment and supplies, he had to get by with a pair of field glasses John had kept from the war. They weren't very powerful, but they allowed him a closer view than mere eyesight. He also missed having his own rifle, but one of the three men he had dispatched owned a Henry and two boxes of shells. Along with some jerky, hardtack and his canteen, that was all he had brought with him.

From the rocky outcrop Rance kept track of the men involved in searching for him. There were four groups,

each having three or four men. After Eva had been discovered on the previous night he had heard shouted
orders and racing horses. Although making a clean
escape, he reasoned Marcone had sent men to cover the
two main routes for getting out of town. That meant
there could be as many as twenty men watching and
looking for him. He wondered how the figure had grown
from the six or eight bandits he had anticipated from
the onset of this hunt. One possibility: a number of the
men recruited for the hunt might be miners or men
from about town. They could have been given a false
story about a dangerous man having killed three of the
local residents – providing the trio had been living in
Wayward. That added a measure of difficulty, as he
didn't wish to harm anyone who was not a part of the
bandit gang.

The morning was long and tedious as he kept watch
and ducked out of sight any time he had a clear view of
one of the hunting parties. Often he saw men on the
ground, walking about, seeking to find his trail.
Fortunately Rance was a professional tracker. He knew
what sign most men could read and how to avoid leaving
those telltale marks or tracks. John had told him only
one of the men was a renowned tracker, a half-Indian
fellow by the name of Red Dog. Fortunately, a man
fitting his description led several men north toward the
old miners' cabin. Most tracks up there would have been
washed away by the rain. Should the man happen across
where he and Eva left the cabin, the trail led to Wayward.
He and the others were searching for a single man on
foot or horseback leaving town in a hurry.

About noon he watched John and his pack animal make their way to the general store. It was one place Bodean had not run out of business or bought. John had known the owner for the year or so he had been in business, so he was a good man from whom to get information. John claimed he and the man often traded gossip by the hour and had played many games of horseshoes together. He hoped to glean enough tidbits from their idle conversation to figure out what exactly was going on.

John returned an hour later with a couple of sacks of supplies loaded on his mule. Had anyone been watching it would seem that he went through the motions of going through his possessions and picking out what he would take with him when he left the country.

Twice, riders from one of the search groups arrived at his cabin. John talked with them both times and allowed them to search around his place. His story about the horses in the corral must have satisfied both teams, because the men left after a few minutes. One man did start up the hill, staring up at the massive boulder but, after a short climb, he dismissed the idea. Rance patted himself on the back for taking a long route up to the rock so as to not leave any visible telltale footprints.

One by one the four hunting parties returned to town. By dark they had a few men posted to watch the trails and two patrols riding in opposing circles about the town to keep watch. Rance used the slower route on his return to his friend's cabin, keeping hidden and again leaving almost no trail.

John had a stew simmering on the stove when Rance

finally arrived.

'Beginning to wonder if I would have to eat alone,' John said. 'You must be slowing down in your old age.'

'Says the man who is down to tossing a flimsy one-pound hammer at birds,' Rance retorted.

'I can still wield my work hammers, pard.' John defended himself.

Rance grinned. 'I only hope your cooking has improved since the war. I remember some of the dog-awful concoctions you threw together sometimes.'

'Ain't my fault if you never acquired the taste for grubs, magpies or hoppers. Man facing starvation has to adapt or die.'

'Please tell me there aren't any grasshoppers, inedible birds or swamp rats in that stew pot.'

John snorted. 'You can relax, sonny boy. I done took into account your sissified eating habits and made it about as bland as a mud pie.'

'So what did you find out in town?'

John dished up a couple tins of stew and filled the coffee cups. He sat down at the table with Rance before he outlined what he had learned.

'The girl is locked in the old smokehouse behind the saloon. The tale spread about her is that she and the Wells, Fargo gent robbed the company. You and the gal were working together and, once they had made good their escape, you showed up and killed him. Marcone and some of his men heard the shot, but when they went to investigate you started banging away at them. Supposedly, you killed three men and got away. The girl was left on foot and sneaked into town to try and steal a

109

horse. That's when she got caught.'

'Pretty good story.'

'They have guards watching the lady from a separate location and a couple more on the door. Be real hard to get her out without ending up in a full-scale war.'

'Any idea what they intend to do with her?'

'My friend didn't know exactly, but he said there's been a lot of talk about her.' John put a meaningful look on Rance. 'It's the kind of gossip a person hears when someone wants to get word out about something. You hear what I'm saying?'

'It's information they want me to know,' Rance deduced.

'Exactly.'

'So what's their plan?'

John took a bite of meat and chewed for a moment. 'They are moving her to Dry Creek first thing in the morning.'

Rance harrumphed. 'I wonder what they really intend to do with her?'

'If Bodean doesn't want any harm to come to your sweetheart, his only option is to make her disappear.'

'It's for certain he won't allow her to talk to the law in Dry Creek or go free.'

'My guess,' John said, 'is that they are going to send her on a long trip . . . about a hundred miles beyond the Mexican border.'

Rance understood what that meant and stared at the untouched food on his plate. 'They're going to sell her into slavery.'

'Be as safe as killing her and there's no dealing with a

dead body.'

'If some of the men are talking, it's because they expect me to try and rescue her on the way to Dry Creek,' he postulated.

'Sure enough, it's a trap of some kind.'

'Did you learn anything else about this trip of hers?'

'Several men are going to escort her, reckon three or four. I figure they are planning a surprise for you too.'

Rance considered the news as he began to eat. The food had no flavor, but he consumed it for the energy he would need. *Four men*, he pondered. That would look like enough, except he had taken out three when they thought him dead. Of course, believing him seriously wounded or dead had given him a huge advantage. Still. . . .

'You do realize they will have more planned than a simple escort,' he told John. 'It has to be a well-thought-out scheme. There will be more of them to deal with.'

'My ma told me I was born in the wee hours of the morning,' John said smugly, 'but not yesterday morning. It's an unmistakable trap.'

'How do you think they will do it?'

John scratched the stubble on his chin. 'They can't send extra riders out in front of the prisoner or you would see them. Same thing if they tried to ride parallel. I figure those fellers will have a couple of men following. Not close enough to be suspect, but in a position where they come a-running and catch you in a crossfire when the shooting starts.'

After discussing options for a bit Rance came up with a plan. It was dangerous for both him and John, but it might work.

'We know the trail they will likely take,' John said, after their discussion. 'Can you deal head on with four gunmen, maybe more?'

'I don't have a choice.'

'What if they have a gun trained on the girl?'

'Then I'll take him first,' Rance vowed.

'We could try and get some help?' John suggested. 'I mean, there are probably a lot of men in Dry Creek who would come to the girl's aid.'

'By the time I got a posse rounded up Eva might be well on her way to the border. We can't afford to take that chance.'

'Then it's you and me, fighting side by side again.' John chuckled. 'Hell, I ain't kilt nobody since the war ended. Hate to lose my edge.'

'You might not have to kill anyone on this rescue,' Rance said.

'Still got a whole passel of gunnies in town, pard. Once we get the girl, then the real fight begins.'

'Any help in Wayward?'

'Maybe a little support, but not much manpower. Bodean took control over nearly every place in town in one way or another. There's even talk he wants to start taxing every business to pay for a couple lawmen. Naturally, they will be men already working for him.'

'Our first priority is to free the girl. Once we get her safely to Dry Creek we'll gather enough men to get the job done in Wayward.'

'We best get some rest,' John said. Then with a grin, 'Being that you're a pal looking for a favor, rather than an invited guest, I know you won't mind sleeping on the floor.'

'After not sleeping worth a hoot last night I could probably sleep standing up.'

John laughed. 'Yeah, it's hell being in love, ain't it?'

'Everything set?' Yancy asked Joe.

'Got the men lined out,' Joe replied. 'Nickles is going to lead the way with three other volunteers and the girl.'

'And the two trailing behind?'

'Ace and Walker, two of our best marksmen.'

'You run into any problems?' Yancy wanted to know.

'Just with my brother,' Joe admitted. 'He wanted to get in on the action, but I told him no.' He groaned. 'Stupid kid. He's the one who shot the agent. That guy had no idea we were here in Wayward. All we needed was for him to believe our guys had come back to find out what happened to the three missing men. Hurst still thought we were leaving the country.'

'Maybe Junior thought the agent could have identified a couple of the boys.'

'Uh-uh, he just wanted to kill somebody. I should have handled it myself,' Joe admitted.

'No, my friend,' Yancy told him. 'We need to turn responsibility over to other guys once in a while. Killing Hurst might have been rash, but it also made certain he would not figure out anything concerning our operation.'

Joe turned to other matters. 'Losing three of our men, and now sending three more with the girl is putting a dent in our gang. Most of the remaining guards in town are men Chuck hired for the saloon. They helped to look for Fayne yesterday, but it was because of the story we made up.'

'They are guns for hire.' Yancy dismissed his concern. 'They do what they're told to earn the money we pay them.'

'Sure, boss,' Joe accepted. 'But I'm worried where they would stand if a marshal and posse came riding into town.'

Yancy begrudgingly admitted his partner was right. 'If our plan works tomorrow, we won't have to worry about a posse or anything else. Once Fayne is dead our problems are solved. We can get on with our lives and start enjoying the money we earn.'

'I'm looking forward to that,' Joe said. 'Yes, sir, I sure hope everything goes as planned.'

CHAPTER EIGHT

Watching the trail from first light, Rance and John were able to deduce Marcone's plan. Four men left town with Eva. She was wearing her riding outfit and had a hood over her head. John pointed out the one rider who worked for Marcone; the others were casino guards. After five minutes two more riders – also Marcone's men – took the same trail.

'Just like a Yankee behind-the-lines patrol,' John commented, once they had determined the strategy. 'Soon as you stop the main group, them two following will swoop down on you from behind.'

'About what we figured,' Rance said. 'Try not to be late.'

John guffawed. 'My being late ain't your worry, pard. You are going to have your hands full.'

The two of them split up and Rance went off on a trail that led around the hill. He pushed his horse at a rapid pace, knowing he had to get to the narrow ridge ahead of Eva and her escort. The terrain was rough, but his replacement horse turned out to be a sure-footed animal. Reaching a ravine, he maneuvered to the bottom and hit the open range below. Rance gave the steed its head and let him run for almost a mile. At that point he turned him toward the mountainous road once more.

He had to proceed slowly once back in the brush and climbing the steep hillside. When he was a short distance from the trail he stopped the horse and tied him off at a fallen tree. Taking the Henry rifle, he quickly moved into position and awaited the party.

Meanwhile, John got ahead of the riders after a much shorter distance. Tethering his mount in a hollow surrounded by chaparral, he left his gun in its holster and moved to a place of concealment. Once the men escorting the girl had passed by he worked his way to a second location closer to the trail. He was prepared to act and was hidden from sight none too soon.

The two riders had their rifles on their hips, and were moving at a steady pace. Their eyes were on the trail ahead; they were being careful not to get too close to the main group. They were ready to bolt forward and go into action at the first sign of trouble.

John remained hidden and let them pass. Soon as their backs were to him, he stepped out behind them. All of the years of practice, of winning bets with his skill, of doing his best under pressure, it all came into play. John swung his arm in an arc and then used the muscle and power of his right arm to launch one of his hammers. Even as it flew a perfect course, he wound up to hurl a second weapon.

He had targeted the man riding slightly behind the

other, due to the trail going between a couple of trees. With branches hanging out over part of the trail, the two could not ride side by side. The hammer made a slight *thump* as it caught the rider right at the base of his skull.

John released the second hammer as the man in the lead turned his head to look back. It was a ghastly mistake on the rider's part. The full weight of the metal-shaping tool smashed against his forehead. Both men were unseated from their mounts and hit the ground like two dropped eggs.

John approached slowly, so as not to frighten the two horses. Both mounts had stopped in confusion at having their riders suddenly fall off. John quickly caught up the reins of the pair and tied them off. He then dragged the two lifeless bodies from the trail, retrieved his hammers and hurried to get his own horse. He knew Rance was proficient in a fight, but four against one constituted steep odds.

The war had taught Rance that the line between bold and foolhardy could usually be measured by the success of a mission. Setting the Henry rifle behind a boulder, within a couple easy steps, Rance moved out to block the trail. He met the five riders with his revolver in hand.

'Sit easy, boys,' he ordered. 'Give me the girl and I'll let you live.'

The warning worked about as well as waving a flag in front of a bull to shoo him away. The man holding the reins to the hostage's horse was the only one who didn't reach for his gun. Rance fired quickly, hitting the man who rode with Marcone in the chest. As he spilled from his saddle the other two cleared leather. Rance fired a well-aimed round at each man. One was hit high in the shoulder and the other caught a slug in his gun-hand wrist. Both of them dropped their pistols and slapped a hand over their injuries. Not one of the trio got off a shot.

'We give up,' the man holding Eva's horse shouted, raising his free hand. 'Hold your fire!'

John came riding up from behind. Rather than a gun, he had a hammer in one hand, ready to throw if necessary. He pulled up short, seeing the fight was already over.

'Silly of me to come running.' He chuckled. 'I thought you might need help.'

'Release the girl,' Rance commanded the guard nearest her.

Instead of turning Eva's horse loose, the man reached over and pulled off her hood. Rance was stunned. It wasn't Eva!

'Who are you?' he asked the girl.

'Belle Freelander,' she said quickly. 'I'm a singer at the saloon.'

The man who had made no effort to join in the gun-fight shrugged a helpless gesture. 'The boss didn't want to risk losing the prisoner. He paid four of us five hundred dollars each to make this ride.'

'Four?'

The guy tipped his head at the man lying on the ground. 'That's one of Marcone's men ... name of Nickles. The rest of us are guards from the saloon.'

'What were the names of the two following?' John

118

wanted to know.

'Also Marcone's men – Walker and Ace.'

'How far were you supposed to go?' Rance queried.

'Only to the river crossing, about halfway to Dry Creek. We were the bait to draw you out.' He swung about, looked at John and shook his head. 'Doesn't appear to have been a very smart plan.'

'I'm bleeding pretty bad here,' one of the wounded men complained.

'This shoulder hurts like hell,' the other one joined in.

Rance waited while John removed the guns of all three men, deciding on what his next play should be. He allowed that Belle could bandage the two wounded men while he and John put their heads together.

'Bodean out-foxed us, old buddy,' John said. 'I kilt those other two for nothing.'

'All three of the dead men worked for Marcone. They were likely part of the bandit gang that killed Corwin. Don't get too sentimental over their demise.'

'Just saying, about all we accomplished was to cut the odds.'

'Come over here.' Rance spoke to the uninjured man. He obeyed while the girl worked to wrap temporary bandages around the two injured men's arms.

'I want the truth,' Rance warned him. 'You give me straight answers and we might just let you live.'

'One lie,' John warned, raising a hammer, 'and I'll flatten you like a bug on a hot rock.'

The guy paled at the threat. 'Ask away,' he said eagerly.

After five minutes with the man known as Lefty, Rance and John again spoke to the girl. She had been hired on as a singer, but was being pressured to offer more intimate favors. She had agreed to ride as a decoy for the money offered.

'What are you going to do now?' Rance asked her.

'Jeff and I . . .' she tipped her head in the direction of Lefty, the man they had previously interrogated, 'we were going to pool our money and buy a little store of our own somewhere. I'm not about to start sitting with and being groped by a bunch of drunken miners. Besides, Jeff thinks Mr Bodean and Joe Marcone are mixed up in something illegal. It seems real fishy about the way they locked up that girl, but didn't want to contact the law. We were trying to figure a way to leave Wayward and this was a perfect opportunity.'

'Lefty said he worked for Lefever.' Rance continued to question her. 'He claims to have never rode with Marcone.'

'Never,' she said. 'Jeff was hired to oversee security for the casino. He's never hurt anyone.'

'What do you think?' Rance asked John.

'Turn 'em loose,' John replied. 'According to Lefty . . .' he grinned, 'or *Jeff*, as the gal calls him, the two wounded men were not part of the hold-up crew. Howsome-whatsoever, the three dead men all rode with Marcone. They are wanted by Wells, Fargo.'

'Where is the girl held prisoner?' Rance questioned Belle.

'Still in the smokehouse, far as I know.' Her eyebrows crested for emphasis. 'I didn't know about her at all until

Chuck had me trade her one of my dresses so I could wear this here riding outfit.' She pulled a face. 'They didn't tell me I would have to ride with a hood over my head until we were ready to leave town.'

'Everything fits,' John said. 'The two men following were supposed to slip up on you while you were trying to get the hostage. They would have killed you for sure.'

'John,' Rance said, 'ride back and pick up the bodies of the two jaspers that were following. We'll send them all to Dry Creek.'

As soon as John had his horse headed back down the trail, Rance waved Lefty back over. He looked hard at the man and was satisfied by what he saw in the man's eyes.

'Marcone and Bodean committed a number of express robberies,' he informed him. 'They also killed a Wells, Fargo agent on this very trail. I intend to take them in . . . alive or dead.'

He let the news set in, then pointed at the two injured men. 'You said these two were not part of Marcone's main gang?'

'That's right,' he said. 'Like me, they were hired as guards for the saloon. We all agreed to ride along on this job because of the big money offered. I'm surprised they went for their guns.' He shrugged. 'Guess it was an automatic response due to Nickles making a grab at his weapon. My first concern was to keep Belle from getting in the way of any flying bullets.'

'All right. This is what I want you to do,' Rance outlined. 'As soon as my friend gets back with the other two bodies you take the dead men and your two wounded pals to Dry Creek. They have a doctor there and you can make a full report of what I've told you to the sheriff.' Then his demeanor turned cold. 'But, so help me, if any one of you tries a double-cross or sends a message to warn Bodean, I will track you down and have you all thrown into prison for robbery and murder.'

'You got my word,' Lefty avowed. 'I'll see that no one talks to the law but me.'

'Tell the sheriff that Corwin Hurst, the Wells, Fargo agent, is dead, and that Ransom Fayne is on the killer's trail. He's to let the guy who is working at the express office know what has happened and get word to the Wells, Fargo headquarters.'

'I'll do exactly as you say.'

A few minutes later John returned with Walker and Ace strapped over the backs of their horses. The wounded had been bandaged and were ready to ride, along with the girl and Lefty. Rance retrieved his horse and rifle before speaking to Lefty one last time.

'Get going,' he ordered. Then, softening his expression, he glanced at the lady. 'Good luck to you both.'

Lefty and Belle led the way. Four riders, two of whom were wounded, and three draped bodies. They would make a curious spectacle when they entered Dry Creek.

'Well, this is a fine turn of events.' John snorted. 'We got rid of three more of Marcone's men, but your girl-friend is still a captive.'

'There's a mystery at play here, John. Several things don't add up.'

'Want to explain your notions, pard, or do we plan a way to get your galfriend out of that cage?'

'You're right. We don't have a lot of time before

Marcone and Bodean expect their men back. I'd guess a few hours at best. Lefty said the remaining men working for Marcone were named Sadler, Topknot and Red Dog. That makes three, plus the Marcone brothers and Yancy Bodean.'

'So we still have six to deal with.' John grinned. 'That sure beats the twelve to fifteen you told me about when we started this here campaign.'

'Except there are still several guards who don't know we are the good guys.'

'I've an idea about that,' John said. 'Care to give a listen?'

'Go.'

Eva's empty stomach told her it was well past breakfast time before the door opened. The blackness of the shed was illuminated with a sun that was already high in the sky. She sheltered her eyes from the brightness as Chuck, again wearing his bowler hat, entered with a plate of food and another jug of water.

'Bet you thought we had forgot about you,' he said weakly. 'I was told you were leaving this morning. I didn't know Joe had made you change clothes until a few minutes ago.'

'At least he was a gentleman about it. He kept his back turned.'

'Good thing it was him and not his younger brother,' Chuck said. 'Junior has morals equal to those of a snake.'

'Where was I supposed to be going?'

'I wasn't told,' he replied, placing the food on the long counter. 'But it looks as if you'll be with us another day or so.'

'I still don't understand,' Eva said. 'Why am I being kept a prisoner?'

Chuck didn't answer, but picked up the empty water jug and retreated toward the door.

'No, wait!' she pleaded. 'Can't you tell me anything?'

Chuck was obviously not used to mistreating or ignoring a woman. Shame spread across his face as he stood with his back to the door.

'I don't know what is going on,' he admitted. 'I only do what I'm told.'

'But you said you were a manager of the casino?'

'Yes, but I don't have control over whatever is happening right now. I supervise the employees at the saloon and oversee the working shifts for the guards. That's all.'

'Do you know what they are going to do with me?'

'No,' he answered, a bit too quickly.

Eva could tell the man was lying. 'Please tell me,' she begged him again. 'It's terrible not knowing the fate that awaits me.'

Chuck shook his head. 'All I can tell you is that you are to be kept safe. Whatever Mr Bodean intends to do with you, he has assured me you won't be harmed.'

'Is there any word about Mr Fayne, the man who accompanied me here?'

'I believe he is the reason one of my girls left this morning wearing your riding outfit. There were a half-dozen men who also rode out. I don't know the details, but I assume it has something to do with capturing your elusive friend.'

'You're working for a bandit, a kidnapper, and a murderer,' she informed him. 'Joe Marcone killed an
employee of Wells, Fargo and kidnapped me.'

Chuck's face contorted into an expression of disbe-
lief. 'I was told that you and a Wells, Fargo agent stole a
pile of money. Once you were a few miles out of town,
your secret love, Ransom Fayne, killed him. Marcone
claims he and some of his men heard the shooting and
went to see what had happened. That's when Fayne
killed three of his men and the two of you got split up.'
He shook his head. 'While he was on the run, you were
caught trying to steal a horse at the livery.'

'What a ridiculous lie!' Eva cried. 'I was hiding in the
barn so I could hear Joe Marcone's voice. I recognized
him as the one who kidnapped me and killed my
brother. I gave away my position when Junior Marcone
bragged how he killed Corwin Hurst, the Wells, Fargo
agent.'

Rather than question her or allow her to continue on
that line, Chuck turned for the door. 'I'm sorry, madam,
I . . . I can't help you.' He threw the last words over his
shoulder as he hurried outside.

Once the door closed Eva was left with only a solitary
candle, a plate of stew, cornbread and bread pudding.
Hunger was again overshadowed by the wild story that
had been made up about her and Fayne. She had to
admit the circumstances fitted, other than for the death
of Nelly. How did Marcone and Bodean intend to
explain her brother's death? It was so bizarre, so out-
landish. No one would believe that Corwin – a member
of the social elite of Dry Creek, a man who made an

excellent income, who aspired to one day be a district manager or – even more – would be involved in a common theft.

Considering her own position again, she tried to make sense of what had happened. *I'm not to be harmed,* Chuck had told her. An idiotic comment, considering she had been kidnapped and held prisoner for two days, not to mention being taken captive and left tied up in a shack with Corwin that first night. Chuck either believed the story about her or preferred to remain ignorant of the crimes committed by Marcone and Bodean. He was a part of it now, helping to keep her locked up.

Forgetting her predicament, she wondered what kind of sinister plan involved using a decoy and someone dressed like her? It had to be a trick to flush out Rance. If he thought she was being moved. . . .

A sudden chill imbued her entire body. The shiver was not for herself or from the ambient temperature. The plan was to ambush Rance. Had it worked? Had he risked his life to rescue her and been drawn into a murderous trap?

Eva took a bite of the bread pudding. It was quite good, but held little interest for her at the moment. She rued the day she had first sat down with Rance. His being a gentleman and allowing her to become acquainted with him might well have cost him his life. He maintained he would have gone after Nelly regardless, once he knew of the robbery. Even if that were true, he would not have been likely to fall into an obvious trap. He was too smart for that, too good at his job. Having her along had caused him to alter his methods, take risks, and get careless. If whatever diabolical plan they had devised worked, Rance might be lying dead or injured at this very moment.

'Dear Lord,' Eva murmured aloud, 'don't let me be responsible for another death. My selfish desire to save Nelly from being labeled a criminal has already cost the life of Corwin. Please don't let Rance die because of me too.'

CHAPTER NINE

Joe entered the office without knocking. Red Dog was right on his heels. Yancy pushed back in his desk chair and waited for the news.

'We're up to our nose in road apples,' Joe lamented. 'Listen to what Red Dog has to say.'

Yancy scowled at the halfbreed. 'Don't tell me the plan failed?'

Red Dog returned a brazen stare. 'I warned Joe that I ought to go along with the main group.'

'Tell me what happened.' Yancy ignored his comment.

'I followed along on my own,' Red Dog began, 'just in case the boys ran into trouble. I figured Fayne might have been watching the town, so I didn't leave until fifteen minutes after Ace and Walker. I heard two or three shots fired a long way off. I thought the plan was working, until I arrived on the scene.'

'So what had happened?' Yancy shouted, his patience gone.

'From the tracks I found, it looks as if Fayne might have come from behind Walker and Ace. I found two different blood patches. Looks as if they were then loaded back on their horses.'

'And the four men with the girl?'

'A quarter-mile further along the trail, I found where all of the animals had stopped and milled about in one place. It was difficult to tell what took place, but I could make out where one body had hit the ground. There was a little blood in another place or two as well.'

'So what does all that mean? Where are the girl and our men now?'

'Gone,' Red Dog said. 'I followed for a bit, until they turned down the main trail. There's no doubt, the whole bunch was headed to Dry Creek.'

'What?' Yancy yelped like a stepped-on pup and sprang to his feet. 'Why would they go there?'

'With so much traffic, I couldn't read their number, at least a half-dozen horses.'

Joe cleared his throat. 'Things are getting totally out of hand, boss. If Fayne took them to the law in Dry Creek, there could be a posse headed up here in a matter of hours.'

Yancy paced back and forth in front of the big office window. 'I can't believe one man could subdue six men.'

'We're talking about Ransom Fayne,' Joe reminded him. 'Most men are not going to try their luck against him.'

'He won't desert the girl,' Yancy reasoned. 'Fayne will come for her.'

'You think he's still close by?' Joe asked.

'Ask the professional hunter,' Yancy snapped, throwing a disgusted glance at Red Dog.

'Being half-Indian doesn't make me Fayne's equal.' The man defended himself. 'He's reputed to be the best tracker in the country. I'm not close to being as good as him.'

'Obviously,' Yancy said sourly.

'What's our next move?' Joe wanted to know.

'The next move is Fayne's.' Yancy whirled about to look through the window to the floor below. 'I imagine he was more than a little miffed at being tricked into rescuing Belle.'

'Wonder why Belle didn't come back?' Joe questioned. 'I mean, why would she and the three saloon guards go along to Dry Creek?'

'Lefty and Belle are more than friends,' Red Dog explained. 'The two of them have been seeing a lot of each other.'

Yancy's jaw dropped. 'When did this happen?'

'No one pays much attention to me,' Red Dog replied. 'I sit back and watch. I see some things you miss from up here in your private lookout.'

'That's why they insisted on being paid up front,' Joe surmised. 'Lefty and Belle are going to strike out on their own someplace else.'

'How does that justify the others all going to Dry Creek?' Yancy demanded to know. 'What is in it for them?'

'Our boys wouldn't have gone there willingly,' Joe averred. 'If Ace, Walker and Nickles went along, they were prisoners.'

'Or dead,' Red Dog tossed out the notion. 'Remember, I found several blood patches. They might all be wounded or dead.'

Joe grunted. 'Damn, boss, this is getting serious. We've lost six men and have nothing to show for it except the body of the Wells, Fargo agent – a guy we hadn't even set out to kill – and a kidnapped woman you don't want harmed.'

'How many of the guards on Lefever's crew can we trust?'

'If you mean going up against the law,' Joe said, 'not a one. Chuck hired mostly men who had tried their hand at mining and had just about starved. The two best men with guns went with Nickles and the others to set a trap for Fayne.'

Yancy pounded a fist into his palm. 'Damn the rotten luck! All of this trouble from one blasted bounty hunter.'

'Ransom Fayne didn't earn his rep by being incompetent,' Joe said.

' 'Breed.' Yancy put his attention on Red Dog, 'I want you to round up Sadler and Topknot. The three of you need to figure out what Fayne will do next and put an end to him.'

'I'll get right on it,' the man promised. 'Like Joe said, the other guards are pretty useless against a real gunman.'

'They can protect the saloon,' Joe spoke up. 'I told Chuck to hire on more guards this morning.'

Without another word Red Dog left the room. Once the door closed Joe stepped over to stand at Yancy's side.

'Maybe we ought to take what money we have and put Nevada behind us, boss.'

'That weasel of a barfly in Dry Creek will be watching.

If there's a posse being mounted, we'll know about it right away.'

'Sure you can trust him?'

'I pay him for information. The man is a petty thief and a town bum, but he enjoys the money. He was quick enough to let us know about the three-man – well, one woman and two men – posse. We'll hear from him once he learns what is up with our missing people. If Lefty goes to the law. . . .' He gave a negative shake of his head.

'Lefty doesn't know a thing about the hold-ups and our men won't talk. When you stop to think about it, there's no real proof against us,' Joe said. 'The only witness is the girl, and we've got her locked up. Fayne hasn't talked to her since we caught her eavesdropping in the barn. That means he can't prove anything either.'

'The best way for this all to go away is to be rid of Fayne. After that, we make the girl disappear like we planned. Without either of those two to point a finger at us, no one can prove that we are anything more than owners of a saloon.'

As was his custom, Joe agreed. 'Right you are, boss. Let's hope Fayne makes a mistake.'

'His weakness for the girl will be his undoing, Joe.'

'I'll let Junior know to keep his eyes open. With Red Dog and our last two boys working to catch or kill Fayne, there's only him and me to keep watch on the rest of the town.'

Yancy bobbed his head. 'Yes, Fayne doesn't know the guards at the smokehouse are ex-miners, so he will still think we have a dozen men.'

'Sure hasn't slowed him down yet,' Joe said.

Yancy didn't offer another word and Joe left the office. Turning his attention to the crowded floor below, Yancy could see men drinking, gambling and socializing with his girls. Losing Belle was a loss, because she had been a fair singer. However, once Fayne was dealt with, he would bring in two or three more who could dance and sing. His dream was still within reach. All they needed was to catch and kill that troublesome bounty hunter.

It was dark outside when the man in the bowler hat arrived with Eva's evening meal. She rose from where she had been sitting on a meat-cutter's stool, determined to try and reason with him. She took a step in his direction, then stopped dead in her tracks.

'How are you holding up, you beautiful doll?' a wonderfully familiar voice asked.

Eva sprang into Rance's arms, nearly dislodging the tray of food. He managed to set it on the counter as her lips attacked his own. She hugged him tightly and kissed him with such passion his legs turned rubbery and he nearly lost his balance.

Eva finally pulled back to look at him, flushed from the heated contact, but with tears glistening in her eyes. 'I've been so worried about you,' she murmured. 'Chuck told me . . .' She ceased what she was going to say and looked at his hat. 'You didn't hurt him?' she questioned him. 'I mean, he isn't a part of Marcone's bandits.'

'I'm here with his blessing,' Rance replied. 'It helped that you had already told him about Marcone and Bodean. Once John confirmed the story, Chuck agreed

133

to work with us. As it was dark out, I borrowed his hat so anyone seeing me would think it was him bringing your meal. John just took over as the guard on your door so you won't have to stay in here much longer.'

'But . . . I mean, how. . . ?'

Rance pulled her close and kissed her again. This time he was ready and both of them experienced the same ardor for a few blissful seconds. Then Rance gently pushed her away and smiled.

'If we continue this cozy reunion much longer, we'd better pick out a name for our firstborn.'

The lady laughed, a musical, wondrous mirth that smothered thoughts of the deadly chore ahead. Rance took a few moments to drink in her outward charm and beauty before he grew serious.

'We've got a plan,' he said. 'If it works out, I'll be bringing you some company.'

'Company?'

'John will explain it in detail. All I can tell you is to trust me.'

Eva flashed a happy expression, as if she could not have frowned if she had tried. 'You must know by now that I trust you with my life.'

'OK,' he said. 'I've got to get moving. The guards John relieved shouldn't return until morning, but Marcone will have his own men on alert. We don't have a lot of time.'

'Be careful,' she warned. 'I don't want to lose you.'

'That's the nicest thing anyone has ever said to me.'

Eva kissed him again, a short, heartfelt contact before pulling back. 'I'll be waiting,' she promised.

Rance went back out into the night. He had a job to do, but, after holding Eva in his arms, he felt he could have roped and branded the moon. Conveniently, John was ready to bring him back down to earth.

'Chuck overheard one of the men say Red Dog and two men are searching for you.'

Rance pondered the new information, then said, 'We'll stick to the plan. With luck, I might get a couple of pigs to market before your relief shows up.'

'Don't get careless, pal o' mine,' John counseled. 'Rumor has it Red Dog is a wily son.'

'You're worried about me?'

The man snorted indifferently. 'I'm worried about myself. I'll be to hell and gone up that proverbial creek if you get yourself killed.'

Junior Marcone was not happy. Joe informed him the hostler was needed to handle guard duty at the saloon. Being short-handed, Junior would be stuck sleeping in the barn for the night. Walking around to squelch his anger, he paused for a few moments, set himself, then drew his gun. He allowed a smirk to curl his lips. He was getting quicker every day. Once Fayne was dealt with he'd stand up to his brother and demand he be put on gun wages. Now that Lefty had skipped out on them, he could take over his job and become ramrod over the casino guards. Do a little drinking, hold a girl on his arm, and tell the bunch of yahoos watching the floor when to work and where to squat.

He smiled at the notion. Yeah, that would be the life. Ever since their pa died, Joe had ridden roughshod over him. *Do this – do that –* like he was a little kid. Well, that was going to end soon enough. He spun the gun around on his finger and slid it neatly back to its holster. *That's right!* he thought. *Joe ain't gonna tell me what to do no more. No, siree. I'm gonna step up chin to chin and tell him. . . .*

'Stay quiet, Junior,' a voice rasped from the shadows. 'You have one chance to live, and that's to do as I say.'

Junior rotated very slowly until he could see a man standing a few feet away, right in front of the first stall.

'Ransom Fayne.' He barely breathed the name.

'I'm cleaning house, Junior,' Rance told him. 'If you want to try your luck, my gun is still in its holster. Just be aware,' he grunted contemptuously, 'I saw you draw just now. You can drop your hardware or make a play and die. Either way, I'm going to take you off my list.'

'What list?'

'The list of men I either have to kill or capture, Junior. I'd prefer to kill you for shooting Corwin Hurst, but the gunshot would force me to play a game of hide-and-seek with Red Dog and the others. You drop iron and I'll put you where you will be safe and won't cause any trouble.'

Junior had his hand on his gun butt. Adrenaline rushed through his veins, pumping up his senses. His heart thundered within his chest. This was his chance. He'd be the biggest man in town if he took Ransom Fayne face to face. He stood poised, his breath coming in short gasps, every nerve in his body alive, pulsating, on edge. . . .

Reality had a way of stomping all over a man's heroic notions. One look at the confident bounty hunter, and Junior's courage was supplanted by a foreboding terror.

He knew, as sure as the sun rose every morning, if he touched his gun he would die. Without mustering a word of defiance, he slid his hand to the buckle of his gunbelt and let his weapon drop to the floor.

Rance quickly tied his hands. Then, picking up the holstered gun and a small hammer, he put a hand on Junior's shoulder and guided him toward the barn's back door.

Eva was surprised when John came through the door with Junior Marcone in tow. Using one of the meat-hooks, he forced Junior's arms up over his head and lifted his bound wrists over the hook. It forced Junior to stand on his toes to take the strain off his wrists.

'Now, little lady,' John instructed Eva. 'I'll demon-strate how you handle this tough *hombre* should he decide to make a fuss or attempt to call out for help.'

'You're both gonna be hanging here before morning,' Junior threatened. 'My brother and Red Dog will—'

John silenced him instantly. It took only a swift rap to the chest with a small hammer.

Junior gasped from the blow and could not draw a breath. His face turned red, visible even in the dim light of the single candle, and the young man sagged heavily on the meat-hook.

'There's a junction of the ribs here in front of a person which shows the location of a body part called the solar plexus – about the same as the pit of the stomach.' John handed the hammer to Eva. 'A smart tap with this tool and Junior won't make any noise.' He grinned. 'Not until he catches his breath, and that can take a little time.'

Junior had gone from red to blue, trying desperately to suck wind into his lungs. He finally managed a slight moan and gulped in a swallow of air.

'Where did you say to hit him?' Eva asked, displaying a wicked smirk. 'There?' She tapped their captive between the ribs.

'A little lower,' John directed.

She was drawing back the hammer for a second try when Junior suddenly found his voice.

'W-wait,' he managed breathlessly. 'I'll be quiet.'

Eva still held the hammer ready. 'I don't know, John. I really ought to keep at it until I can hit the mark every time.'

'I swear!' Junior cried. 'I won't make a peep.'

Eva still feigned another strike, causing Junior to jerk back and lose his footing. He swung helpless for a moment before he got his feet under him again.

John led Eva to the door and kept his voice down. 'I'll be outside. If anything should happen, you keep Junior quiet. So long as no one knows there's anyone in here but you, you ought to be safe.'

'How many men are still out there?' she asked. 'Can you and Rance handle them all?'

'With Chuck pitching in, I was able to relieve the guard on the roof before I came down and relieved the two on the door. Rance wore Chuck's hat in case any of Marcone's men happened to see him coming here. We're getting the odds down to a manageable level.'

'Be careful,' she said.

John went back out the door. Once it was locked tight, Eva went over to the plate of food. With all of the excitement she had little appetite, but she wanted to keep her strength up. There was no way of knowing what would happen next.

CHAPTER TEN

The town runner hurried up to Joe and handed him a message. 'For Mr. Bodean. Just arrived from Dry Creek,' the young man said. 'Knew you'd want to see it right away.'

Joe took the message and tossed the kid a dollar. The boy waved his thanks and hurried back out of the saloon. Joe didn't bother to read the telegram, but promptly made his way upstairs. He found Yancy at his usual spot, sitting behind his desk where, with a turn of his head, he could keep an eye on the floor of the casino.

'Telegrapher sent this over just now. I imagine it explains why no one got back to us about our trap.'

Yancy put his hands together, locking his fingers. 'Read it to me.'

'It says three men are dead and the saloon guards won't be coming back. Two were wounded and Lefty and Belle bought stage tickets to the nearest railroad station. It looks like they are leaving together to start over in some place new.'

'Ace, Nickles and Walker are all dead?'

'So it seems,' Joe replied. 'The wire also says that two of the dead men had their heads caved in.'

That bit of news caused Yancy to sit up straight. 'What?'

'Like they had been hit with a . . .' Joe crushed the paper in his hand, his face darkening with a sudden fury. 'Holy hell, boss! Kegan asked for his hammers from the livery. He's working with Fayne.'

'Find Red Dog and let the others know,' Yancy directed. 'Get everyone after that blacksmith. We find him, we find our bounty hunter.'

'I'll see to it,' Joe said, spinning about. He hurried out of the office and bolted down the stairs. He should have foreseen this. John Kegan had once shown him how accurately he could toss a hammer, when he killed a snake that had spooked a couple of horses. Thirty feet or more away and he had crushed its head with a single throw.

Outside the saloon, he decided the quickest way to find Red Dog was to check with the guards and see if they knew where he was searching. He looked at the top of the adjacent building, where one sentry was supposed to be watching.

Nothing.

With a renewed rush of fear entering his being, Joe went to the alleyway and strode briskly to the smoke-house. He about fell on his face when he saw John Kegan guarding the door. The man had his heavy jacket buttoned up against the evening chill and held a rifle in his hands. Looking around slowly, Joe didn't see anyone else. That meant Fayne was working on some kind of scheme elsewhere. Convinced John was alone, he moved forward in a normal walk.

'Kegan,' he said amiably, as if surprised. 'Chuck hired you?'

'The pay is good,' the blacksmith replied. 'As I don't have my business any more, I can use the extra money. I reckon I'll stick around for a few more days.'

Joe continued to move toward him. When he was within two steps he quickly drew his gun. Pointing the muzzle at Kegan, he growled, 'Where's the bounty hunter?'

John feigned shock. 'What are you talking about, Marcone?'

'I know you're working with him.'

John dropped his rifle and backed away. 'You're buckin' against the wind, Marcone,' he warned him. 'Give it up now and you can live through this.'

'Fayne is only one man.'

'That one man has cut your gang in half. Do you really think you have a chance of beating him?'

'Guess you'll never know.' Joe pulled the trigger.

John grabbed his middle, staggered a couple steps backwards and collapsed.

Joe knew the ex-blacksmith would die a hard death, having shot him in the stomach, but he deserved to suffer. He'd help kill Ace, Walker and Nickles. Turning his attention to the smokehouse, he pushed open the door, gun still ready for instant use.

'Help!' Junior cried like a woman in labor. 'Don't let her—'

There came a muffled gasp as Joe pushed the door

wide and tried to penetrate the darkness. With only a candle showing, it took a moment to see the girl. She was standing next to his brother, who was hung up like a side of beef. Even from fifteen feet away he could see a twisted grimace on Junior's face. His mouth was wide open, struggling to draw in a breath of air.

'Get away from him and drop that hammer,' Joe ordered Evangeline. 'What are you doing to him?'

'He isn't hurt,' she muttered curtly. 'It's a little trick John showed me, to keep a man quiet.'

'I've had a time or or two where knowledge like that would have come in handy.'

Junior, still trying to inhale a bit of air, skewed his expression at Joe's levity.

'Back up into the corner while I get my brother down,' Joe told the girl. 'We're going to move you to the saloon for safe keeping.'

'I heard a shot.' Fear was strong in the girl's voice. 'You didn't kill Rance?'

'Red Dog will get him,' Joe said confidently, untying Junior's hands. 'I took care of your blacksmith pal.'

Grief swept over her features and Eva's eyes misted with tears. 'You killed my brother, you killed Corwin; and now John. How many people are you willing to murder for your blood money?'

'Just one more, honey,' he told her. 'Soon as Fayne is taken care of, this will all be over.'

'And me?'

'Yancy has plans for you which, I'm sorry to say, doesn't include killing you. I think that's a mistake, but he's the boss.'

143

'And you would have no qualms about killing a woman,' she stated.

'None,' he told her bluntly. 'That's why you'd best do exactly as I say.' He spotted Junior's gun and holster on the cutting counter and gestured to Junior. 'Strap on your iron and find Red Dog. Tell him they only have to worry about Fayne.'

Junior hurried to do as he was told, but stopped at the door and paused to look at Joe. 'Thought you shot Kegan? Where's his body?'

'He probably crawled off to a hole somewhere,' Joe said back. 'I put a slug square in his breadbasket. He's gonna suffer long and hard before he dies.'

Junior disappeared and Eva stared at Joe with a cold, hard gaze. 'I won't be sorry when Rance ends the lives of you and your brother, Mr Marcone. You both deserve to die for your crimes.'

'You wait for him to save you,' Joe challenged, 'and I'll wait for news that he is dead. We should know by morning who backed the wrong horse.'

Rance heard a shot just after he spotted three men moving in the dark. He worried that the gunshot might have come from the smokehouse, but he didn't dare lose sight of Marcone's men. He recognized the man in the lead as Red Dog, so he kept out of sight and followed the trio. When they reached the barn they called out for Junior.

'Where do you think he went?' one of the men asked when they got no answer.

'Worthless as udders on a boar,' Red Dog growled.

144

'You'll have to take the other side of town on your own,
Topknot.'

'No problem,' the man he spoke to answered. 'I'll
keep to the shadows.'

'Me and Sadler will do a sweep around the far side
and then go by the smokehouse. We'll meet you at the
tavern in fifteen minutes.'

Topknot left and went across the street. Rance backed
up far enough to make the crossing without drawing
attention. Still wearing the bowler hat, he hurried to cut
the man off before he reached the rear of the saloon.

With the vague light coming from the lamps in the
nearby buildings, Topknot recognized the bowler hat
and stopped as Rance approached.

'What're you doing out here, Chuck?' he asked. 'Are
we so short of guards that you're taking a turn on watch?'

Rance drew his gun before the bandit member could
see his face. 'One sound,' he warned him in an icy tone
of voice. 'One wrong move and the next thing you see
will be the underside of six feet of dirt.'

'Ah, damn!' Topknot whined, though he didn't say it
loud enough to sound an alarm. 'Wearing that stupid
hat, I mistook you for Chuck.'

'Be glad it wasn't a fatal mistake,' Rance said. 'Now
turn around.'

With his pistol in the man's back, Rance removed
Topknot's gun. The man remained perfectly still until
his gun was lifted from its holster. Then he spoke over
his shoulder.

'I swear to you, Fayne, I had no part in the kidnapping
of the lady or killing that Wells, Fargo agent. I helped

with the express robberies, but I've never hurt no one.'

'That could help with your defense,' Rance said, giving him a nudge to start him walking.

'No,' Topknot retorted, after going a short way. 'I mean it. I never joined the gang to be part of kidnapping or murder. My cousin, Digger, is the one who got me mixed up in this.. We grew up together in Texas and went and fought against the Yanks. After the war we just wandered here and there until Digger met Joe. He said he had a job that would pay big money. Me and Digger was going to go back to Texas, once we had enough money to buy us a place.'

'So why didn't you?'

The man sighed. 'We haven't been paid for our last job yet. Digger volunteered to ride with Marcone when he got a wire saying you were on his trail.'

'A wire?'

'Yeah, Bodean hired some no-account drunk to keep an eye on Wells, Fargo in Dry Creek. He sent a message that you, a woman and the agent were following. I didn't want no part of it, but Digger said the money was too good to pass up.' He snorted his contempt. 'Then he goes and gets himself kilt. He was one of those three you shot when they came back to check on you after the ambush.'

'But you didn't ride with them?'

'I stayed in town the whole time. Like I said, I didn't want to be a part of anything like that.'

'Being involved in several robberies is enough to get you a couple years in prison.'

Topknot bobbed his head. 'And I'd sure enough

accept punishment for that, but I ain't no kidnapper or murderer. I don't want to hang for what these other guys have done.'

They had moved close enough to see the smoke-house, but John wasn't there. No one was guarding the door. Taking another few steps, Rance saw the door was not even closed all the way.

'Hold it.'

'Must have been Marcone,' Topknot offered. 'I seen the kid who runs messages for the telegrapher a few minutes ago. He was headed for the saloon with a piece of paper in his hand.'

'Bodean's snoop-dog must have seen the wounds on the dead men,' Rance postulated. 'John took out two of them with his hammers.'

'Hammers?'

'Man can throw a hammer close fifty to sixty feet and nail about any target you can put up.'

'Listen, Fayne,' Topknot made a plea. 'I don't want any part of this. You turn me loose and I'm gone. You'll never hear of me getting involved in anything illegal again.'

'How do I know I can trust you?'

'Because I'm gonna tell you a way to get to Bodean without anyone seeing you.'

Rance sighed. 'I'm in a fix here, Topknot. John has been captured or killed and the girl is gone. If you swear to me as a Texas Confederate that you'll do as you promise and tell me straight about how to get to Bodean, I'll let you go.'

'I swear by both the Confederate and Union flag,'

Topknot vowed. 'I ain't certain what they done with Kegan, but I'd wager they took the girl up to Belle's room. It has a lock on the door – all of the doors for the girls have locks, as a safety measure.'

'You said there's a way to get up there without being seen?'

'Most people only know about the main stairway, but there is a second way upstairs.'

'I'm listening.'

'That's him!' Junior pointed excitedly. 'The bounty hunter is still wearing that bowler hat.'

Fayne was exiting the barn, but he moved deep into the shadows and was gone.

'Someone is leaving town on a horse,' Sadler observed. 'Who could that be?'

Red Dog grunted his disgust. 'Topknot. The yellow coyote is running out on us.'

'Do we go straight after Fayne?' Junior wanted to know.

Red Dog resisted the urge. If Fayne spotted them first, he might just kill all three of them. There was a lot of open space between the dry-goods store, next to which they were standing, and the livery. He quickly devised a plan.

'Fayne is on the wrong side of town. Topknot likely told him the gal would have been taken to the saloon. He has no choice but to cross the street.'

'Yeah,' Sadler growled. 'Topknot sure enough sold us out. If I ever see him again, I'll put a bullet in his brain.'

'It does help us to anticipate Fayne's next move,' Red

Dog countered.

Sadler snorted. 'Yeah, so what's our next move?'

'Junior,' Red Dog ordered, 'you go around back of the bakery. Use the alleyway and slip up to the sidewalk. Me and Sadler will come at Fayne from front and back. By the time he sees one of us, we should all be in place.' He cautioned the other two. 'Just be sure of your target. We don't want one of us to get killed by a stray bullet.'

Red Dog sent Sadler in the direction of the livery, where he was to swing wide and come in from behind Fayne. As Junior would soon be ready at the bakery, Red Dog moved parallel to where Fayne should be. He guessed the bounty hunter would cross the street before going very far in order to avoid the bright lights from the casino windows.

He spied a shadow and figured it was his prey. To keep from showing himself, he raced between two buildings and returned via the alleyway next to the walk. He eased forward to the corner of the dry-goods store and stopped dead in his tracks. Fayne was no longer in sight.

Pulling his gun, Red Dog remained frozen within the darkness, fearful any movement on his part would alert the man-hunter. *He's got to be still over there,* he told himself. No way the man could have just vanished.

Sadler appeared at the end of the street. He searched the area with a steady perusal, until he located Red Dog. He lifted his hands in a helpless gesture, curious as to where Fayne had gone.

Red Dog ducked low and moved over as far as a watering trough, using it for cover. He tried to penetrate the blackness of the night with wary circumspection, but saw

149

nothing. Fayne must have moved at exactly the same time as he had. Now he was either hidden in the vacant building across the street, or he had gone down an alley and was behind one of the buildings. That made sense. Topknot probably warned him about the search. Fayne was being careful. A wise gunfighter would pick out a spot where he could watch the street and not expose his position until he knew where Red Dog and Sadler were at.

Red Dog remained hunkered down behind the trough while he signaled to Sadler to leave the livery and make his way to the empty building. Once the man began to move, Red Dog made a hasty dash back to the passageway. He flattened himself against the wall of the dry-goods store and once more scanned the opposite side of the street for any movement at all.

Beads of perspiration formed on his forehead and his heart was racing. He had killed a good many men, but never one as crafty and experienced as Fayne. Where could he have gone?

Sadler reached the vacant building, removed his hat, and cautiously peered through a paneless window. After a few agonizingly slow seconds he returned his headgear. With gun in hand, he went along the outside wall until he reached the rear. He stopped at the back corner and peeked around it for a long time. Once satisfied no one was lying in wait, he disappeared around the back.

Meanwhile, Junior was growing impatient. He showed himself at the front corner of the bakery, trying to figure out what was going on. Red Dog signaled to him to cross the street and move toward Sadler. The landscape behind those few buildings was open for no less than a hundred yards. Fayne wouldn't expose himself out in the open, so he had to be between the two men.

Suddenly, there came a muffled *thud*, followed immediately by a grunt, as if someone had been hit with something. Red Dog sprinted from concealment to cross the street. Fayne had given away his position and made a fatal mistake. They had him now!

CHAPTER ELEVEN

Red Dog had taken about four running strides when a man suddenly appeared in his path. It was Fayne! He immediately dug in his heels to stop and brought his gun up to fire. The flash from the muzzle of Fayne's gun told him he was a split second too late!

An invisible force drove a white-hot spike through his chest. As the echo of a gunshot rang in his ears, his feet went out from under him and his gun was lost. Red Dog didn't recall hitting the ground, but numbly realized he was on his back, staring at the night sky overhead. There came the sound of several shots being fired, but they meant nothing to Red Dog. He felt his life ebb away, seeping out of his body along with the warm wetness of the blood soaking his shirt. A face came into focus as a man hovered above him.

'You should have held your position,' Fayne said. His voice was far away and fading fast. 'I lost track of you until you came rushing out into the open.'

'Greenhorn mistake there,' Red Dog barely whispered. 'I should have. . . .' But the breath of life had left his body.

'Junior threw a few wild shots,' John spoke up, 'then ran like a branded calf for the saloon.'

Rance looked at his friend, who had come to join him. 'Do you think he knew he was shooting at you?'

John laughed. 'Hell, I'm a dead man, remember? 'Bout the only thing he could see was this silly bowler hat you had me wearing.'

'You're lucky Joe wanted to make you suffer,' Rance said. 'If he'd shot you in the heart or head. . . .'

John nodded his agreement. 'Did knock the wind out of me,' he said. 'That bullet of his drove one of my hammers right into my gizzard. I thought I had been shot for a bit.'

'Good thing you crawled away,' Rance said. 'He might have checked on you otherwise.'

'So we stick to the plan?'

'What about Sadler?'

'Not to worry,' John replied. 'I give him a little tap on the noggin, but I never had a gentle touch. He'll likely sleep the night through.'

'Let's put Red Dog's body and Sadler in the smoke-house. Then you get into position and we'll finish this.'

Joe and Yancy were in the upstairs office when Junior came running through the batwing doors. His eyes were wide and a naked fear shone on his face. Pushing through the crowd, he raced up the stairs and burst through the door.

'They's dead!' he cried like a hysterical woman. 'Red

Dog, Sadler . . . that bounty hunter is a ghost! He's every-where! And nowhere!'

'We heard some shooting.' Joe tried to calm his brother. 'Tell us what happened.'

Junior shook his head, staring around the room as if he'd wandered into a maze. 'We . . . we set the trap,' he said, gaining some control over his panic. 'But Fayne took out Sadler without firing his gun. I seen him fall and ran to get a shot at him. Red Dog came a-running from a different direction. Then I hear Fayne shoot Red Dog – yet he is right there before my eyes, coming for me. I emptied my gun at him, but the guy is made of shadows. The bullets must've gone right through him.'

'You're ranting like a frightened child, Junior,' Yancy scolded him. 'You probably didn't come close to hitting him. Where is Topknot?'

'We saw a rider leaving town. Red Dog figured it was him.'

Joe stepped between the two of them. 'Topknot never wanted anything to do with grabbing the girl or killing anyone. With Digger dead, he lit out to save his own hide. That means there is just the three of us left.'

Yancy turned and looked down at the busy floor of the casino. No one seemed interested in the shooting that had taken place out on the street. They likely figured it was some drunk letting off a little steam. Searching the two security positions, he saw that the guards were in place. Chuck was off in a corner, talking to a man who was holding a mug of beer, wearing a long buffalo robe and a severely weathered beaver hat. Even as he watched, Chuck left the man and went to the back of the casino.

The hunter plopped down at an empty table, his back to the office, and sipped at his drink.

'What'll be do?' Junior could not prevent his voice from squeaking with trepidation. 'Fayne's gonna come for us.'

'We've still got the woman.' Joe attempted to soothe his panicked brother. 'He doesn't know where she is and he can't get to us up here. If he comes through that front door, we'll cut him down before he reaches the stairs. There's no place for him to hide.'

'Maybe he won't come,' Junior said. 'What if he waits us out? We have to go outside sometime.'

'Joe,' Yancy took charge, 'you take up a position at the bottom of the stairs. Junior can set up at the top. I'll keep watch and shout a warning if the man shows his face.'

'J-just the two of us?' Junior whined.

'If Fayne comes in here with a gun out, let out a yell and the guards will open fire.'

Joe took hold of Junior's arm. 'Let's get in position. Even if he manages to get past me, you'll have a clean shot at him on the stairs. Don't miss!'

Yancy returned to his vigil at the window. Chuck was on the floor again, speaking to some of the customers. He had a friendly smile on his face as he moved through the crowd. Unable to stand the suspense, Yancy went to his cabinet and poured himself a drink. He sank down on the sofa, took a few swallows of courage, and leaned back with his eyes closed.

This was it. Either they killed Fayne or all of his dreams were dust. One man . . . one diehard, never-quit, bloodhound of a man. Damn. Everything hinged on the bounty hunter's life or death.

Rance entered through the rear door of the saloon, the one Chuck had unlocked for him. He kept out of sight and found his way to the small area behind the stage. There were cords and ropes for extra lights and curtains, plus a catwalk high overhead. Yancy had certainly spared no expense. This saloon and casino had a set-up that would handle a traveling roadshow of 'most any size.

Climbing up the ladder to the narrow platform, Rance crossed to an access panel which opened into an upstairs supply closet. He maneuvered past the linen and cleaning supplies, eased his gun out of its holster and slowly opened the door to the second-story hallway. There were several rooms to either side, but no guard in sight.

Rance quietly tried each door and found they were all unlocked and empty, except for the large office and one other room. He tapped lightly at that room, whispered, 'Eva, are you in there?' and put his ear to the door.

'I'm here!' she called back at once. 'The door is locked; I don't have the key.'

Rance didn't risk breaking down the door . . . not yet. 'I'll be right back,' he said softly.

Junior was sitting on the top step of the stairs with a shotgun across his lap. His eyes were on the batwing doors and the floor of the casino. Rance took a deep breath and let it out slowly. The time had come to finish this job.

'You should have left town,' Rance announced, loud

enough for Junior to hear. 'Turn and fight or throw down the scattergun.'

Junior scrambled to his feet in such a hurry the shotgun slipped out of his grasp and went spinning down several steps.

'Everyone outside!' Chuck abruptly shouted. 'Get out now!'

Every man, woman, guard, dealer or barkeep vanished in a matter of seconds . . . all but one.

Joe hadn't heard the gun fall but, at Chuck's yell to clear the room, he turned to bolt up the stairs. He didn't make it, however. John shrugged out of the heavy buffalo robe with a hammer raised.

'Shoot me again,' he called to Joe, and released a deadly accurate throw.

Joe rotated about, his right side halfway around, when the hammer slammed into his upper arm, near the top of the shoulder. The force of the blow knocked him right off his feet. He lay there writhing in pain from his shattered arm, as John marched over and removed his gun.

'Clear down here, pard!' John bellowed up to Rance.

Junior had not the slightest inclination to fight. For the second time, he hastily unhitched his gunbelt and threw up his hands.

'Downstairs with your brother,' Rance ordered. 'The two of you can hang, along with Sadler.'

Rance waited until John had both men covered. The entire place had emptied, including the guards, all courtesy of Chuck having warned everyone ahead of time. He looked down at his friend and called, 'Toss me a hammer!' John did so and Rance caught the perfectly pitched tool.

Going down the hallway to the locked room, he first warned Eva to stand back. Then he used the hammer to destroy the lock and bash open the door. Eva came into his arms and kissed him. Rance held her for a few wonderful moments, then pushed her back to arm's length and regarded her with a serious gaze.

'It's up to you to get Yancy Bodean to open his office door, Eva. I don't want to kill him.'

A puzzled frown sprang to her face. 'Why should he listen to me?'

Rance sighed, wishing there was an easy way to tell her. Sympathetically, he said, 'I believe Yancy and your brother are one in the same.'

'What?' She was stunned. 'That's not possible! I saw his body!'

'Strange, isn't it,' Rance countered, 'that Joe and the others would take time to throw dirt over a body – a body you and Corwin would have covered the next morning on your own?' Before she could answer, he continued, 'And why would he order his men to kill me, then murder a Wells, Fargo agent, and yet not harm you? Killing Corwin meant a major manhunt, including the hiring of Pinkerton men. The gang had nothing to lose by killing you.'

'But . . . but. . . .' Eva was confounded beyond speech.

'Call out to him,' Rance directed her gently. 'Call out to your brother.'

Eva approached the office door in a daze. 'Nelly?' she managed, swallowing a sob of fear and regret. 'Nelly, is that you?'

Only silence.

'Nelly?' she tried a second time. 'Please. Are you there?'

'Damn it, sis,' Nelson responded in a resigned tone of voice. 'Why did you have to get involved in all this?'

'I can't believe you stole that money, that you are a robber, a . . . a murderer and a thief,' she sobbed. 'Why?'

'You ruined everything,' he responded without answering her question. 'You and your man-hunting pal. The plan was perfect. No one would ever have connected me to Yancy Bodean. I would have had everything I ever wanted.'

'By stealing and killing!' she cried. 'What kind of monster are you?'

'The kind who takes defeat lying down,' he muttered. 'Time for you to claim your bounty, sis.'

Before she could ask what he meant, a gunshot sounded from inside the office. Rance used the hammer and busted the door open. Nelson was lying in a pool of his own blood, with a mortal wound to his temple. A short distance away the huge safe door was ajar.

'You ready to ride back to Dry Creek?' Rance asked Eva. 'The two guards Chuck provided have our three prisoners ready for transport.'

She gave an affirmative nod, but could not hide her anguish. 'Seems a shame to bury Nelly here in Wayward, but it's where he wanted to be.'

'John said he would look after his grave,' Rance said. 'He has taken back the livery and kept the money Joe paid him – claimed it was little enough payment for all his trouble.'

'Chuck promised he would look after the saloon until I got the deed changed over to my name.' She grimaced. 'I never imagined owning a casino.'

'Prettiest saloon owner in the country,' Rance teased.

'Well, we first have to figure out how much we owe to Wells, Fargo. Fortunately, Chuck claims the place is making a lot of money.'

'The jewelry was in the safe, along with over thirty thousand dollars,' Rance summed up. 'Ten per cent for returning the money and another eight hundred dollars for each of the bandits. I figure we will own the place free and clear.'

'So we start out with a saloon as my dowry?'

He laughed. 'Just until Chuck can get a loan and take over the ownership. Then you and I can start a new life . . . wherever you like.'

Eva kissed him tenderly and then pulled back to smile at Rance. 'We can make that decision together. That's what a husband and wife do . . . isn't it?'

Rance grinned. 'I still think you're too good for me.'

Eva laughed. 'Good. That means you will work that much harder to make sure I'm happy.' With a flirtatious wink, 'And I'll do the same for you.'

Rance and Eva began their walk toward the livery. It was a great feeling, having her on his arm, knowing his bounty-hunting days were over. Life was meant to be more than tracking down bandits and criminals. With the right woman at his side, they had a good life ahead. Who could ask for more than that?